"We are more
than merely
Lucian, Janus,
Ekaterina, Tomas,
and Madrigal.
We are all Cahills,
and we are
under attack."

CAHILLS vs. VESPERS
THE MEDUSA PLOT

GORDON KORMAN

SCHOLASTIC INC.

NEW YORK TORONTO LONDON AUCKLAND
SYDNEY MEXICO CITY NEW DELHI HONG KONG

For Charles Isaac Korman, who continues
to put up with all this. —G.K.

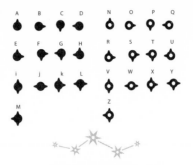

Library of Congress Control Number: 2011922487

ISBN: 978-0-545-32409-0

10 9 8 7 6 5 4 3 2 1   11 12 13 14 15

Book design by SJI Associates, Inc.
Book illustrations by Charice Silverman, Keirsten Geise, and Rainne Wu
"The Head of Medusa" pg. 66 (c) akg-images/Electa/The Image Works

Library edition, August 2011

Printed in China   62

Scholastic US: 557 Broadway • New York, NY 10012
Scholastic Canada: 604 King Street West • Toronto, ON M5V 1E1
Scholastic New Zealand Limited: Private Bag 94407 • Greenmount, Manukau 2141
Scholastic UK Ltd.: Euston House • 24 Eversholt Street • London NW1 1DB

PROLOGUE

Napa Valley, California, 5:42 A.M., Pacific Time Zone

Fiske Cahill loved the early morning — the glorious moment when the sun's rays broke over the mountaintops. He would always be an easterner, but there was no place quite like California.

He eased himself into the mineral bath, feeling the bracing sting of water heated by magma trapped deep within the earth. The ache and stiffness of his sixty-nine-year-old body seemed to melt away, and he knew complete relaxation and contentment. Nothing could spoil the perfection of this moment.

He closed his eyes. That was his first mistake.

There was a tiny splash as the snake hit the water. It was a water moccasin, a baby — the venom is strongest in the very young.

Fiske never saw it. He was aware of a sudden stab, followed by blinding pain and then blackness.

Two men in coveralls lifted him out of the tub and administered a tiny injection of antivenom to his abdomen. Then they wrapped him up in a vinyl pool cover, carried him to a panel truck, and loaded him inside.

As an afterthought, one of the men fished the snake out of the water and tossed it into some tall grass. If it survived and happened to bite another resort guest, it was no concern of theirs.

Ponce, Puerto Rico, 9:42 A.M., Atlantic Time Zone

Long, powerful strokes propelled Reagan Holt through the sparkling Caribbean. At thirteen, she had already completed seven Ironman triathlons, but now she was training for the world championships. Puerto Rico's lesser-known southern coast was the ideal place for it — great weather, uncrowded roads for running and cycling, and warm, crystal-clear water for swimming. There was even entertainment for these grueling ocean marathons. Through her goggles, she enjoyed the floor show: hundreds of fish species, colorful coral, and . . .

A jolt of surprise threw off her rhythm, and she struggled to maintain her textbook form. At first she thought it was an undersea mirage, but no. Twenty yards away, a few feet below the surface, floated a scuba diver in an antishark cage!

What's going on?

That was when she saw the hammerhead.

It was big—an eighteen footer at least. It moved in a serpentine pattern, its oddly placed eyes sweeping the reef. When its attention locked on Reagan, she knew instantly. The long body became a guided missile hurtling toward her. Panic was immediate and total. Not even the fastest human could outswim a shark.

The cage. It was her only option. She made for it, expecting at any moment to feel the devastating bite of jagged teeth. The diver read her mind and opened the cage door. She flung herself inside, slamming the gate shut behind her just as the hammer-shaped snout smashed into the titanium bars. The very sea itself seemed to shake. Reagan was thrown back against the frame, but the structure held.

The diver pulled on a signal rope, and a mechanical winch began to lift the cage out of the water. As they broke the surface, she spied the boat. Relief flooded over her. The cost of this training session would not be her life.

Crew members swung them in over the gunwale and set them down on the deck.

It was all Reagan could do to maintain her footing as she stepped onto the wood planking. "Thanks, you guys! That was so close—"

And then she noticed that one of the sailors was pointing a gun at her.

London, UK, 1:42 P.M., Greenwich Mean Time Zone

When anyone advised Natalie Kabra to "find a happy place," that place was always Harrods.

That was the reason for this mental health day away from her boarding school. When the going gets tough, the tough go shopping. And where better than the most famous department store in the world, located in the heart of London's Knightsbridge?

A glance at a bus-stand billboard took the wind out of her sails. It was an advertisement for AidWorksWonders, a nonprofit organization dedicated to global disaster relief. Peering compassionately out was the organization's founder, radiating charity, goodwill, and kindness.

Natalie didn't believe it for a second, and she was in a position to know. That woman, Isabel Kabra, was Natalie's mother—a hard-hearted, cold-blooded conspirator, arsonist, murderer, and terrorist. The only reason she had formed an organization that did good in the world was that it had been her ticket out of jail, to parole and community service. Natalie pitied the poor community Isabel was assigned to serve.

Just the sight of her mother almost made her turn around and go back to school. It had been Mum who had first introduced her to Harrods. But one couldn't blame Harrods for that, Natalie concluded, stepping in through the brass-plated revolving door.

Muscle memory took her directly to the Girls' department — designer only, of course. Without once consulting a price tag, she collected an armload of outfits and headed for the fitting room. She stepped inside, wondering at the second click that came a moment after she shut the door. She tried the handle. Locked.

And then her world tilted, dropping her against the mirror. The entire cubicle lifted suddenly and began to move forward.

In the Girls' department, the shoppers paid little attention to the large box being carried out of the department by two employees in Harrods uniforms. No one heard the screams that could not penetrate the soundproof enclosure.

Paris, France, 2:42 P.M., Central European Time Zone

To Nellie Gomez, Les Fraises was the best sidewalk café in Paris, and she had tried most of them.

Nellie adored Paris. As much as she missed home, this monthlong class in French cuisine was a dream come true. She loved living in a place where nose rings and punk-rock hair and makeup were considered completely normal. She loved the sights of the city, from the ancient Roman ruins to the ultramodern glass pyramid entrance to the Louvre.

But mostly, she loved the food. Her seminar on sauces had run through lunch, which gave her the perfect excuse to visit Les Fraises in the state she was usually in—hungry.

The chocolate-strawberry croissant looked a little different as the waitress placed the plate on the table next to her espresso. Was that confectioner's sugar on top? Was the chef trying to improve upon perfection? She was anxious to find out.

Nellie raised the pastry to her lips.

Poof!

A cloud of powder burst from the croissant, enveloping her face. It was gone in a few seconds. But by then, Nellie was slumped in her seat, unconscious.

An ambulance pulled up to the café. Two white-coated attendants emerged. They lifted Nellie out from behind the table, loaded her into the back, and drove away.

Tel Aviv, Israel, 3:42 P.M., Israel Standard Time Zone

"This way, children."

Alistair Oh held out his arm and guided Ned and Ted Starling into the elevator of the medical office building. How tragic it was that Alistair, at sixty-six, would be offering his assistance to two teenagers in the very prime of youth and strength. It should have been the other way around.

Alas, such was the legacy of the search for the 39

Clues. The boys had been victims of a cowardly act of sabotage at the Franklin Institute in Philadelphia. Ned now suffered headaches of such intensity that he could not concentrate for more than a few minutes at a time. He was the lucky one. His brother was legally blind.

Alistair sighed. Perhaps Dr. Shallit could help. That was the purpose of their trip to Israel—to see the foremost neurologist in the world. He had achieved miraculous results for patients with similar injuries.

Alistair pressed the button, and the elevator began to ascend. At the eighteenth floor, the car slowed and stopped.

The door did not open.

The next thing he knew, they were dropping, free-falling down the elevator shaft, picking up speed.

"Children—" The word died on his lips. There was nothing reassuring to say about plummeting two hundred feet to a violent death.

He tightened his grip on the boys' forearms. What an odd place for their lives to end. Yet it was somehow fitting that members of the same family branch should perish together.

In the space of a few vertical feet, the elevator went from terminal velocity to a dead stop. The sudden deceleration flattened all three of them to the floor. Ned bumped his head and cried out in pain and fear.

The door opened. Three large men blocked the entrance to the underground parking garage, their faces obscured by desert head scarves. The leader reached down to grab Alistair. He underestimated the older man's determination. Alistair's diamond-handled cane came up and fractured the man's wrist.

The attacker cursed and withdrew in pain.

Alistair boosted the boys to their feet. *"Run!"* he ordered.

Ned took his blind brother's arm, ducked beneath the hands that were reaching for them, and took off down a long row of cars. One of the assailants followed in hot pursuit.

They were almost at the exit when Ted stubbed his foot against a cement parking curbstone. He never hit the floor. Their pursuer grabbed him in a powerful bear hug.

Ned hesitated as the onslaught of another headache shattered everything in his mind except pain.

No. Not now—

With almost superhuman effort, he turned back to his brother. Ted was caught, and Alistair was subdued back at the elevator. Only he was free.

Alistair's voice echoed in the concrete space. "Go! Call William McIntyre!"

With a heavy heart, Ned Starling fled.

Tokyo, Japan, 10:42 P.M., Japan Standard Time Zone

Phoenix Wizard was searching for the hip-hop vibe.

That's what his cousin Jonah had told him to look for. It should have been easy to find in a crowd of screaming fans, all jumping, stomping, and shouting along with Jonah Wizard, the number one recording artist on the planet.

The teenage rapper was spectacular. From the upper decks of the enormous stadium he must have appeared insect-size on the stage far below. And yet every move, every beat, every "wassup, yo" sent ripples through the audience. Jonah was a hip-hop hypnotist, and all sixty-five thousand people in the arena were obeying his commands — to get wild, get loud, get *down*.

Except one.

Phoenix worshipped his A-list cousin. What twelve-year-old boy wouldn't idolize a celebrity? And Jonah wasn't just famous in the music world. He had starred in several movies, including *Gangsta Kronikles*, his first blockbuster; he had his own reality TV show. His face was immortalized on PEZ dispensers and motorized lollipop holders. Paparazzi followed him everywhere.

Yet the music — that was the part that left Phoenix flat. He would have cut his tongue out before saying it aloud, but he thought it was truly awful. Just talking, really. Bragging in time to a simple repeating beat.

Why can't I see what all these people see?

Jonah began to whip up the crowd to even greater heights. "I love Tokyo — it's the only place where 'yo' is part of the name of the town! *Get up and show me some moves!*"

The response was seismic. Those fans who weren't already standing rose to their feet in a wave of tens of thousands of bodies. Phoenix was up with them, hoping that their enthusiasm was contagious.

He felt nothing. What could be more pathetic than a Wizard with no rhythm? All around him, people were gyrating as if their very lives depended on it. He watched, amazed, as bodies were lifted up and rolled across the top of the crowd, passing from hand to hand.

A teen girl floated over him, her expression sheer bliss. *She* had found the hip-hop vibe.

Determined to share the experience, he climbed onto the armrest of his seat, literally hoisting himself onto the "roof" of the audience. He felt a thrill when he started to move, twirling as he skimmed above the concertgoers' heads. For some reason, there was no fear. The thousands of hands created a seamless surface. It was almost like swimming — riding ocean currents around the stadium. This was awesome! He couldn't wait to tell Jonah about it after the concert.

And the ride was getting better! He seemed to be picking up speed. But why was he heading away from the stage toward one of the exit tunnels? That wasn't where the action was!

Then he was down out of the throng, in the darkness of the concrete passage, flanked by two men in mirrored sunglasses.

"What—?"

A foul-smelling wet cloth covered his face. He attempted to struggle, but one whiff of the chloroform brought oblivion.

Although they took place in different time zones throughout the world, the kidnappings were executed at exactly the same moment. The victims had only one thing in common: All seven were members of the Cahill clan, the most powerful family in human history.

CHAPTER 1

A branch had found its way up Dan's sleeve and was tickling his armpit, but it was totally worth it. From the tree, he was looking straight down on the porch swing by the patio doors. There sat his sister, Amy, next to her boyfriend, Evan Tolliver. This was going to be good. They had only been dating for a few months, but Amy had been obsessing over this guy for the past two years. Talk about a match made in heaven—the library nerd and the computer geek. He tapped the button to activate the sound recorder on his cell phone. Posterity had to know the exquisite words of romance that were about to pass between this Juliet and her loving Romeo.

Come on, people, I don't have all day! The school bus will be here in ten minutes!

Determined not to miss a single word—if there was ever going to be one—he inched forward on the branch, perched precariously above the couple.

The first sound that met his ears was certainly not an expression of love.

"Mrrp."

Dan risked a glance over his shoulder. Sitting behind him on the same branch was Saladin, the much-pampered cat Amy and Dan had inherited from their grandmother, Grace Cahill. The Egyptian Mau's green, inscrutable gaze skewered him like twin lasers. In his mouth, Saladin carried an empty tin of Russian caviar, his latest favorite snack.

"Not now, Saladin!" Dan whispered. "Can't you see I'm busy?"

The cat regarded him solemnly and began to stroll out onto the branch.

"Back off!" Dan hissed. "You'll get us both killed!"

Saladin was no lightweight, thanks to his expensive taste for caviar, fresh red snapper, shrimp dumplings, and sushi. The branch was beginning to tremble.

In an attempt to restore balance, Dan shifted his weight. That was all the limb could take. With a crack, it tore away from the tree. Saladin leaped for the trunk and held on with his claws. The branch and Dan dropped as one unit, sprawling at the feet of the couple on the porch swing.

Amy and Evan shot out of the double seat, staring down at Dan amid the wreckage.

"Were you spying on us?" Amy demanded.

Dan picked himself up, brushing at a cut on his arm. "I was trying to coax Saladin out of the tree with some of that caviar he likes," he explained, his face the picture of innocence.

Saladin interjected an outraged *"Mrrp!"* and the tin fell to the ground.

"And you can stay up there until you've learned your lesson!" Dan scolded the cat.

With an exasperated sigh, Amy shinnied up the trunk, wrapped her free hand around Saladin's big belly, and clambered down again, setting the Egyptian Mau on the lawn. Dan noted the ease with which his sister scaled the tricky maple. She was an athlete now. That was something new. She trained constantly — running, rock climbing, working out like a maniac in their basement gym. It was the same old Amy, yet not quite. Two years before, she had been soft, timid, and unprepared when fate had unexpectedly required extraordinary things of two Boston orphans. So she had been preparing.

Dan felt the threat, too, but his sister had based her entire life on it.

Amy shook her head in disgust. "Just because you've elevated dweeb-hood to a fine art doesn't give you the right to snoop on the rest of us. Don't you have anything better to do?"

Dan glared back at her, stung. He could never tell her the truth. He *didn't* have anything better to do.

Amy hadn't been the only one crisscrossing the globe on a high-stakes treasure hunt two years before. Dan had been with her every step of the way — living by their wits, a split second ahead of disaster, with nothing less than the future of the world on the line.

The 39 Clues. Two years ago, he'd never even heard the term. But, by the end of their grandmother's funeral, he'd learned more than he'd ever wanted to know. He and Amy were part of the most influential family in history. The source of their power was hidden in the Clues.

The Clue hunt had stretched them to the limit of human endurance. It had shredded their very souls. It had very nearly gotten them both killed.

So why did it feel like it had been the only part of Dan's life that meant anything?

When you've been through something like the clue hunt, the eighth grade just doesn't measure up. How could it?

Drag yourself out of bed. Get on the school bus. Do homework. Repeat fifty thousand times.

Not that Dan wanted to return to being chased, blown up, shot at, punched, poisoned, strangled, and used as crocodile bait. It had been awful. Go back to that? Never!

And yet he had never felt so keenly alive as he had during those crazed, perilous weeks. Lately, Dan had become fascinated by stories of soldiers returning home from the horrors of war. They were thrilled to be out of it. Yet they struggled to fit back into their families and routines.

On the surface, Dan had everything he'd ever wanted. They were rich. They lived in a huge mansion with every video game, gadget, and entertainment system in existence. He had a degree of independence and freedom most thirteen-year-olds only dreamed about.

So what was the problem? Why did he feel like his world was coming out of a tinny twelve-inch black-and-white TV built in 1967?

Maybe I'm just bored. . . .

Either way something was missing.

A series of flashes from the opposite end of the estate caught his attention. He squinted to see Sinead Starling in the window of the guest cottage, angling a hand mirror into the sun.

"Hey, isn't that Morse code?" Evan asked.

"It's probably that Soviet cold-war code she just broke," said Amy. "That's her new favorite."

"Why does she need *any* code?" Dan grumbled. "She lives in our guest house. She can talk to us any time she wants."

He already knew the answer. Tall, strikingly pretty, and brilliant, Sinead never did anything the easy way. She had turned down the genius grant from the MacArthur Foundation to fix up the guest house and join Amy's personal boot camp. They had been bitter rivals during the Clue hunt, yet in no time at all, the two had become as close as sisters.

Sinead was cool, Dan had to admit—for a person with a favorite code.

The flashes ceased and Sinead emerged from the small home. She hopped onto a four-wheel ATV and roared across the rolling property up to Amy, Dan, and Evan. A pair of welder's goggles was pushed off her forehead into her mane of auburn hair.

"The school bus is running early," she reported. "I was up on the roof, and I saw it coming down the highway."

"Why were you on the roof?" asked Evan.

"I'm retrofitting the furnace for zero carbon emissions, and I had to make a few chimney modifications. You guys should really let me take a crack at that monster in Grace's house. Your energy efficiency is pathetic."

Everyone still called the main residence Grace's house after Amy and Dan's grandmother, even though Grace herself had never lived there. The original mansion had been destroyed by fire right after her funeral. Amy and Dan had rebuilt it from pictures and loving memory. From the outside, it was as close to the original as they could possibly make it—a haven and a place of happiness for two orphans. Inside was another story: infrared cameras, Geiger counters, bulletproof windows. And those were just the security features.

They heard the roar of an engine followed by the screech of an ancient transmission as the bus geared down approaching their gate. Evan took Amy's wrist and began to escort her toward the road.

Can those two do anything without touching? Dan reflected, falling in behind them. The constant hand-holding irritated him. Ditto the arms around shoulders, hanging off each other, and general

THE MEDUSA PLOT

17

closeness. It was like a spotlight on his isolation.

"See you later," Amy told Sinead.

Sinead didn't attend school. The education system had more to learn from her than vice versa.

Her mind was still on furnace modifications. "I could cut your heating bill by two-thirds."

"We're loaded, remember?" Dan retorted.

"Global warming doesn't care what's in your bank account," she called after them. "Think it over."

The bus lurched to a halt and the door folded open. The three hustled down the long drive and boarded.

Dan found an empty row of seats and slumped across it. On both sides of the aisle, pairs of friends jabbered excitedly about sports and TV and books and the day ahead.

Not Dan. For him, this was the most pointless part of a routine that was less than awesome to begin with. Why would two kids with enough money to buy thirty Maseratis take the bus to school?

He would never understand it. If they ever created a school transit exhibit in the Smithsonian, the bus to Attleboro Junior/Senior High would be prominently displayed. It was old; it was hot; it was overcrowded; it smelled. Shock absorbers? What shock absorbers? Every bump and pothole vibrated up and down his spine.

Amy said it was necessary. They had to blend in. Right—like that was going to happen. During the Clue hunt, he and Amy had seen and done things—awful things no kid should even know about. They had memories that would never fade. It was especially true for Dan. . . .

He checked his cell phone. 8:40 A.M. School hadn't even started yet, and he was already counting the minutes before he could go home. If real life felt lame after all he'd been through, that went double for Attleboro Junior High.

He regarded his sister a few rows ahead. Yep—she and Evan were doing The Lean. It reminded Dan of a house of cards. Pull either one away and the other would probably drop like a stone. He wasn't sure why they bugged him so much. By all rights, he should be happy for Amy. Her crush on Evan dated back to freshman year. She was so shy it was a miracle she'd ever mustered the courage to talk to him. But now that they were finally dating, they were in their own little world. They probably didn't even notice the grinding gears, the popping springs, and the earsplitting roar of the engine as the bus struggled to stay ahead of the cement truck directly behind it.

Dan frowned. The mixer was really close—only a few feet off the bus's rear bumper.

What's wrong with that driver? Doesn't he know how dangerous it is to tailgate?

The thought had barely crossed Dan's mind when the truck put on a burst of speed and slammed right into the back of the bus.

It was 8:42 A.M. Eastern Standard Time, exactly the

same instant as the Cahill kidnappings around the world.

The impact knocked Evan out of his seat and dumped Amy on top of him. Shouts and cries from all around indicated that other students had been shaken up as well.

A split second later, the tanker truck in front squealed its tires as it pulled broadside, blocking the road. The bus driver slammed on the brakes. Smoke from burning rubber darkened the windshield.

Amy shut her eyes, expecting a collision and a devastating explosion. But the bus lurched to a halt mere inches from the tanker's silver shell.

"Everybody off!" ordered the driver.

The passengers didn't have to be ordered twice. They ran out quickly.

Evan took Amy's hand. "Come on, let's get out of here!"

Amy looked back and confirmed that Dan was unhurt and in line behind them. Then she followed Evan down the bus's front steps.

She noticed two things immediately: 1) The cement truck driver was wearing a ski mask, revealing only his eyes, and 2) those eyes locked on her the instant she appeared.

It's happening. . . .

She had always known it would, but now that the situation was upon her, it was still a shock.

The man took something out of the pocket of his ski jacket. The rush of adrenaline was something Amy had not felt for two solid years. When the hand came up, holding a pistol, her foot was already flying forward. As she kicked the gun out of his grip, she could feel at least two of his fingers breaking. The weapon hit the ground and slid under the tanker and out of reach.

The students scattered in terror. The attacker reached for Amy with his good hand. Evan tried to step in front of his girlfriend and was yanked roughly out of the way.

But Amy was ready. She had been preparing for this moment since the end of the Clue hunt. This was why she'd gotten in shape and trained in martial arts.

She landed two quick punches, which rocked her assailant but did not knock him down. He came after her again, and this time he had backup. The driver and passenger of the tanker, also in ski masks, joined the fight.

Amy kept them at bay, punching and kicking with windmill speed and force. Still, she knew it was a losing battle. She was exhausting herself, and any one of her opponents had much more physical strength than she did.

What will they do to me? she thought in terror. *To Dan?*

In the Cahill world, the consequences of failure were usually severe.

"Amy — stand back!" came a voice over her shoulder.

Dan. She obeyed without hesitation, an instinct from the Clue hunt—the dozens of times he had saved her life and she had saved his.

Dan stepped forward, brandishing the hose from the tanker truck. He squeezed the trigger and soaked the three masked men from head to toe. Then he looked around at the shocked and silent students.

"Anybody got a match?"

The driver of the school bus pulled out a disposable lighter and tossed it to him.

That was enough for the three men in ski masks. They turned and ran, disappearing into the woods that fringed the road.

There was a deafening silence. Nobody moved a muscle. When the students finally found their voices, the frightened questions came in a cascade:

"Who *were* those guys?"

"Do you think they'll come back?"

"Amy—where'd you learn to fight like that?"

"I—I—" Amy tried to speak up, but her stammer got in the way, as it always did in times of stress. Cahill matters had rained down on them before—but never in front of dozens of neighbors and schoolmates.

In front of Evan!

And speaking of Evan . . .

"Dan"—her boyfriend's voice was hushed—"were you really going to do it?"

Dan's legs seemed to collapse beneath him in slow

motion, and he sat down cross-legged in the middle of the road, the lighter still clenched in his fist. He registered shock, yet the look on his face was determined and stone-cold.

Amy knew him better than anyone in the world, but even she couldn't read his thoughts. Sometimes her brother was the same old Dan, who tried to collect everything from bottle caps to Egyptian mummies. But since the Clue hunt, there were times when he withdrew from her and could not be reached.

The Cahills' eyes locked—an exchange of pure anguish. They did not understand the reason for the attack on their school bus. But one thing was certain—those men had been after her and Dan. It was their Cahill history coming back to haunt them.

It had begun again.

The police sirens brought everyone back from speculation and into reality. Being scared to death was no excuse for revealing Cahill secrets. Brother and sister wordlessly agreed that there was only one thing they could not tell: the truth. Obviously, there was a busload of witnesses and a cement mixer and tanker truck that they couldn't wish away. But the next query—the *why*—was not up for discussion.

Cahill business was for Cahills only.

Not only were they the most powerful family of all time, the Cahills were also one of the most tragic. Both their incredible success and their terrible misfortune stemmed from the same source—the 39 Clues.

The Clues had turned out to be the thirty-nine ingredients of a remarkable serum that delivered enhanced intelligence, cunning, creativity, inventiveness, and physical strength to anyone brave enough to swallow it. On the surface, it offered the promise of a better human race. The reality, however, had been much more sinister.

The miracle formula had touched off a blood-spattered quest to control it. It had been nothing short of war between the five family branches — Lucian, Janus, Ekaterina, Tomas, and Madrigal. No one knew how many lives the Clue hunt had claimed over the centuries, from Gideon Cahill himself in 1507, to Amy and Dan's parents in a horrific case of arson nine years ago. It had to be in the thousands.

Now the Clue hunt was over. Two years before, Amy and Dan had united with young members of all the Cahill family branches to destroy the serum outright. No one should have such power. The mere knowledge that the formula existed had turned the Cahills into ruthless murderers. They had put an end to five centuries of madness.

Yet Amy had always waited for the other shoe to drop. Peace and harmony had never been the Cahill way. She had a feeling that today's attack was the first shot in the next war. And this one would make the Clue hunt seem like a stroll on Boston Common.

CHAPTER 2

While the police combed the woods for the three flee-ing bus-jackers, the detective squad took statements from the dozens of young witnesses.

After about an hour, parents were called to take their kids home.

"Ames—" Evan approached his girlfriend. "Tell me what went on back there."

Amy's heart sank. She wasn't sure she ever could have gotten back to a normal life if it hadn't been for Evan. The transition from the Clue hunt to a regular high school had been a rough landing. The only part of it that seemed one hundred percent natural was the way she felt about Evan.

She'd first noticed him in the computer lab, where he held court. He was the Bill Gates of Attleboro Junior/Senior High, but Amy privately assigned him the nickname Adorkable. He was a living, breathing contradiction—deep blue eyes obscured by Coke-bottle glasses; broad shoulders held in a stance that somehow always reminded her of the Pink Panther.

Back then, he hadn't known she was alive, but she'd gradually worn him down. According to Dan, it was the most courageous and decisive thing she'd ever done, next to the Clue hunt. He was probably right. Dan was a dweeb, but he had a knack for cutting to the heart of the matter.

Very little was ordinary about Cahills, and that was especially true of her and Dan. Two orphans, raised by nannies, thrown blindly into the clan warfare of the 39 Clues. Their current situation was more comfortable, but still unusual. As Grace Cahill's heirs, they were rich. On paper, their legal guardians were Uncle Fiske — Grace's brother — and Nellie Gomez, their former au pair. But for all intents and purposes, Amy and Dan were raising themselves.

Evan had no idea of Amy's Cahill ancestry. He had never heard the words *Clue hunt*. He knew she was wealthy — the magnificent house and property spoke for themselves. Yet to him, Cahill was nothing more than his girlfriend's last name.

Until this morning, when I went Special Forces on the school bus.

"You saw what I saw," she answered him carefully. "We may never find out what those guys were really after." She hoped he didn't notice that she wasn't looking him in the eye.

Evan was persistent. "Who taught you those fighting skills?"

"You know Sinead and I have been studying kung

fu." She smiled wanly. "Don't worry, I won't use any of it on you. Jujitsu, maybe."

It didn't bring the desired laugh. "Come on. You kicked a gun out of the guy's hand! And I don't even want to think about what Dan almost did!"

"They attacked us," Amy said stiffly. "We fought back. Anybody would have done it."

"But 'anybody' wouldn't have been so *good* at it!"

Dan interrupted their exchange. "Let's go, Amy. The police are going to give us a ride home."

"I'll go with you guys," Evan volunteered. "I don't want you to be alone. I know Nellie's still in France and your Uncle Fiske is on vacation."

Amy gave his hand a squeeze. "You're sweet. But we'll be fine. I'll call you."

In the car, Detective Corelli had some advice. "I know who your grandmother was, and I know your family's got money. Take my advice—hire yourselves some good security people. This looks to me like someone was trying to grab you kids for ransom. We'll put extra patrol cars in your area, but our manpower is limited. You want full-time protection."

He took his passengers' silence to mean that they were terrified, and added kindly, "I know this sort of thing doesn't happen to kids like you."

Amy and Dan exchanged a look. During the Clue hunt, "this sort of thing" had happened to them constantly.

The cruiser turned onto the large private

driveway of Grace's house.

In the backseat of the cruiser, Dan nudged Amy. "Look," he whispered. "McIntyre's car."

Sure enough, behind their custom SUV on the circular drive was the sleek black Lincoln owned by William McIntyre, their grandmother's lawyer and adviser, and now theirs.

Amy frowned. "How does he know something's up? The school couldn't have called him. Fiske and Nellie are listed as our guardians, not him."

Corelli stopped at the imposing front entrance. "Okay, you two. Home sweet home. We'll let you know when we catch those guys. Meanwhile, stay inside. Anything you're not sure of"—he held out a card—"call."

The Cahills thanked him and entered the big house. They did not get one step inside the foyer before William McIntyre was upon them, his lined face full of relief.

"Thank goodness you're safe!"

Dan was mystified. "How did you find out what happened?"

"I didn't. I merely deduced from events around the world that an attempt might have been made to kidnap one or both of you."

Amy was instantly alert. "Around the world?"

The lawyer ushered them into the old-fashioned Victorian parlor, where Saladin held court atop a stack of cushions that looked very much like a throne. He issued a stately *Mrrp* of greeting.

"Early this morning," McIntyre said grimly, "Fiske Cahill disappeared from the El Rancho Jojoba Spa in California."

"Well," Dan began, "you know Fiske—"

"He was last observed wearing a bathing suit, approaching the hot tubs. All his belongings—including his cell phone—are still in his room." The lawyer's expression was grave. "There's more, I'm afraid. Much more. At around the same time as the last known sighting of Fiske, Reagan Holt went out on a training swim in the Caribbean and never came back. Natalie Kabra was reported missing from her boarding school. They traced her as far as Harrods in London, and there the trail ended. And in Tokyo, young Phoenix Wizard vanished from one of his cousin's—shall we say *livelier*—concerts, right under the collective nose of Jonah's security—what is the word?"

"Posse," Dan supplied, distracted.

Amy was profoundly shocked. "A little over an hour ago, our bus was attacked by three men in ski masks. They definitely knew me, and probably Dan, too. We fought them off, but it could have gone either way."

"Like if they'd used a cookie truck instead of a gas tanker," Dan added. "Nobody's scared of Oreos."

"The police think they were after ransom," Amy went on. "I was half hoping they were right. Now we know better."

"Yeah, but that's *all* we know!" Dan exclaimed in agitation. "Everybody we care about is disappearing!"

There was frantic pounding at the door, and in burst Sinead. Her usual expression of calm control was gone. She looked like she'd been pulled the wrong way through a hedge, her cheeks flushed, her eyes wide.

"Ned just called from Tel Aviv! Ted and Alistair have been kidnapped!" *Kidnapped!* The word echoed through the large room. So many disappearances in so many places—it couldn't be a coincidence. Someone was kidnapping Cahills.

Sinead grew even more upset when the others just stared at her. "Well, aren't you going to *say* anything? Don't you even *care*?"

"Sinead, we've got some news that you should hear." Amy told her friend about the incidents around the globe and the attempt on herself and Dan. "Ned's our first real witness," she finished. "Now we know for sure we're dealing with kidnapping."

"Hallelujah," Dan said sarcastically. "With that and a buck you can buy a lottery ticket. Now tell me something useful, like who these kidnappers are and what they want! Or why us! Or who's next—"

All at once, the thought flashed between brother and sister like radar.

"Nellie!" they chorused in perfect unison.

With the practiced motion of a Wild West gunslinger, Dan had his phone out of his pocket and was speed-dialing the mobile number of their former au pair in Paris.

The furrows in Dan's brow deepened as he listened to ring after ring. "She's not picking up."

Amy detected a panicked edge to his voice and knew he was scared, even though he'd die before admitting it.

"Just because there's no answer doesn't mean she's been kidnapped," Sinead reasoned.

"She answers *my* calls," Dan replied stiffly. "I have my own ringtone on her cell—the Misfits cover of 'Monster Mash.'"

McIntyre flipped open his own phone. "I'll get to the bottom of this," he vowed. "We Cahills have connections everywhere—even inside the Académie Gastronomique."

The lawyer stepped into the kitchen and a nervous silence fell in the parlor.

Sinead was still trying to be reassuring. "Maybe she's in class and her cell is set on vibrate."

It made perfect sense. Yet all the logic in the world could not diminish their growing dismay.

A few minutes later, McIntyre was back. "Miss Gomez fainted at a sidewalk café in Paris. She was picked up by an ambulance that never reported to any area hospital."

"No!" Dan exclaimed in anguish.

Amy's hands flew to her lips to staunch her exhalation of horror.

Nellie had been kidnapped. She was in danger.

Amy had been only seven, and Dan barely four,

when their parents had died. Nellie was the closest thing to a parent they'd had since the fire that had taken Arthur Trent and Hope Cahill away from them.

McIntyre took in their desolate expressions. "While I share your worry, I must remind you that panic will not help our loved ones—especially when we don't yet understand what is happening, and who is behind it."

The four fell silent, listening to the clattering blades that signaled the approach of a helicopter. The sound grew louder and louder until the crystal chandelier began to buzz and vibrate.

"To the basement!" ordered McIntyre. "Quickly!"

But as they rushed to the cellar door, all four caught sight of a small parachute drifting lazily down past the lead-paned windows. As it settled its payload in a hedge of emerald cedars, the helicopter noise grew fainter and finally disappeared.

"It could be a bomb," Sinead suggested nervously.

"If they wanted to kill us," Amy pointed out, "they could have dropped it right on the house."

"I'm going to get it," said Dan. He ran outside, the others close behind him.

The package was about the size of half a shoe box, a canvas bag wrapped in waterproof plastic. McIntyre detached it from the chute by cutting the strings with his pocketknife. Then he removed the plastic cover and unfurled the canvas. Out tumbled a wad of bubble wrap. Amy caught it before it hit the ground and began to remove the tape and unwind the plastic.

"A phone?" Dan queried. "At least I think that's what it is. It sure doesn't look like any phone I've ever seen."

Amy turned the device over in her hands. "There's no brand name or model number."

"Nothing that can be traced," McIntyre noted.

Sinead produced a Swiss Army knife. "I'll open it up, examine the guts. Maybe we can tell something from the way it's wired. And the chip might be stamped with an identifier—"

"Don't you dare," Dan interrupted. "If somebody takes the trouble to parachute a cell phone down on your front lawn, it's because they're going to *call*."

He pressed the power switch, and the device lit up, booting itself to life. There was a chime, and a text message appeared on the small screen.

Greetings, Amy and Dan Cahill.

I'd hoped to meet you in person, but perhaps it's better this way.

Congratulations on your escape from my team. Interesting that Dan chose not to use his lighter. A fundamental difference between him and me. Nevertheless, you have proven yourselves worthy of the task I now present to you.

After you succeed, I will release Reagan
Holt, Phoenix Wizard, Natalie Kabra, Ted
Starling, Alistair Oh, Nellie Gomez, and
your dear Uncle Fiske. Until then, they
will remain with me as a guarantee of
your cooperation.

If you do not arrive in Florence, Italy,
by tomorrow morning, one Cahill will die.
If police are alerted, one Cahill will
die. If my instructions are not followed
to the letter, one Cahill will die. We
hold only seven. You do the math.

You will hear from me upon your arrival
in Florence. Have a pleasant journey.

Vesper One

Vesper. Amy's and Dan's eyes locked. That was the
unspoken name behind all Amy's training and preparation. A centuries-old adversary shrouded in mystery.
She'd known the Vespers would be coming.

Her fingers worked like pistons on the phone's tiny
keyboard: Offer to trade myself for hostages.

She pressed SEND, and the phone responded:
Recipient unknown.

She tried again: Must meet to discuss terms.
Recipient unknown.

"Neat trick," Dan remarked. "That Vesper guy can reach us, but we can't reach him."

Sinead was mystified. "What's a Vesper?"

Amy took a deep breath. "We tangled with them a couple of years ago. I'd hoped it was a one-time thing."

"Yeah, and I believe in the Tooth Fairy, too," mourned Dan.

Amy touched her watch, which had been custom made from a family heirloom — a gold ring. She could never think of the Vespers without reaching for it. It had become an instinctive reaction.

William McIntyre's face was gray. "Come back inside, and I'll tell you what I know. It isn't much, I'm afraid. Not when there are lives at stake."

When they were settled in the parlor, nestled in the velvet upholstery, the lawyer began to speak.

"The Cahills are the most powerful family in history, but that doesn't mean we are without rivals. Five hundred years ago, in the time of Gideon Cahill, there was a man named Damien Vesper — a formidable man, a peer of our illustrious ancestor, but a man with a dark side."

"Like Gideon had no dark side," Dan scoffed. "He only cooked up the juice that almost got us all killed."

"Maybe so," McIntyre agreed. "Yet Gideon had been searching for a cure for the plague when he made his unfortunate creation. Damien Vesper was not so interested in the good of humankind. He, too, was a great alchemist. The nature of his research, however, was far more destructive."

"Like what?" Dan asked, accepting Saladin onto his lap.

The lawyer shrugged. "Sadly, that information has been lost. Or perhaps we never had it."

Amy's brow furrowed. "But the Vespers aren't his descendants, right? Aren't they more like a secret society?"

"A secret society of pond scum," Dan added.

"True, the Vespers are not a family but a cadre of ruthless associates," the lawyer confirmed. "Still, some believe that there may yet be direct descendants of Damien among their number. They are ruled by a Council of Six, dedicated to fulfilling Damien Vesper's dream — whatever that might have been."

"That still doesn't explain the most important thing," Dan pointed out. "Why us? What good does it do the Vespers if we go to Italy? I don't know what this Damien guy was working on. Do you?"

"Don't you see?" McIntyre replied. "The clue hunt is over. Vesper One must believe that you two have captured the serum."

"Then why doesn't he just ask for it?" Amy challenged.

"That I cannot answer," the lawyer admitted. "We know only the barest bones of our situation — that our mortal enemies have kidnapped the people we love in order to bend us to their will."

"I don't love Natalie Kabra so much," Dan grumbled. "And I've only met the little Wizard kid a couple of times—"

"Dan!" his sister exploded. "Of course we're going!"

"I know that. I'm just pulling your chain."

"I'll go with you," Sinead volunteered.

Amy brightened. "That would be great! Thanks, Sinead."

Dan wasn't so sure. "If we're getting ordered around Italy, shouldn't somebody stay here to hold down the fort?"

"Very wise," the lawyer agreed. "Another concern—news of the kidnappings will spread rapidly within the family. You have to reach out to as many as you can to avoid chaos and panic."

Amy looked worried. "Couldn't you do that?"

McIntyre shook his head. "I don't have the authority."

"And we *do*?" she cried in astonishment.

"No one commands the Cahills," the lawyer acknowledged. "Even Gideon himself could not control his own children. This, as much as the serum, is the reason why the branches of our family have been feuding for five hundred years. Only one thing holds sway with us—the thirty-nine clues."

Dan made a face. "You mean we won the clue hunt, so we have to do it?"

"Lucky us," sighed Amy.

CHAPTER 3

Another one of the features that was different from Grace's original house was the communication and command center in the attic. Amy had designed it, insisting that it could serve as a kind of Cahill headquarters in an emergency.

Dan had petitioned to turn the space into an indoor paintball battlefield. Now, he reflected ruefully, it was a good thing Amy had won that argument. And, he had to admit, no paintball battlefield, or laser-tag arena, or even the greatest video arcade on the planet could come close to the amazing array of high-tech gadgetry on display here. The dome, for example. It was a working astronomical observatory keeping track of *Gideon*, the Cahill satellite with spy capabilities. *Gideon* provided near-perfect reception on the three dozen high-definition video monitors. The only interference: sunspots. Sinead was already working on solving that.

The babble of voices made Dan's head hurt. Thirty-six screens, thirty-six agitated Cahills, and thirty-six wildly different opinions on what had to be done—immediately. Tears from Leila Wizard, Phoenix's mother. Blind rage from the Holts, Reagan's family. Genuine distress from Ian Kabra, Natalie's brother, but also cold calculation.

On monitor 27 (Asia/Oceana), Jonah Wizard's normally confident features were warped into an expression of deep concern as he pleaded with his aunt on monitor 11 (Southwestern USA).

"Leila, you can't call the cops! Vesper One said no police, and the dude's not playing!"

"I'm supposed to do nothing when my little boy has been abducted?" Phoenix's mother demanded.

Amy tried to step in. "You're supposed to leave it in our hands. We're the ones the Vespers contacted."

She could not have anticipated the acid of Leila's reaction. "And who are you, exactly? A sixteen-year-old child."

"She's a Madrigal, that's who she is!" Eisenhower Holt had only one volume setting—loud. "I never trusted them before, and I'm sure not about to start now! How do we know they're not behind these kidnappings? I never heard of any Vesper!"

Ned Starling spoke up on 22 (West Asia/Middle East). "It's happening to all the branches, not just the Tomas," he said from Dr. Shallit's clinic in Tel Aviv, where he'd been accepted as an inpatient. "You should have seen the guys who grabbed Alistair and Ted! They meant business—" He had more to say, but a wave of pain contorted his face and erased his train of thought.

Amy fought valiantly to control the conversation and her deepening stammer. "It'll be better for R-Rea — it'll be better for Reagan if we k-keep our heads —"

She's losing it, Dan thought, leaning against the wall, a little apart from the action. Not that he could do better. Nobody could. To unite bickering Cahills was like trying to make something out of pieces from a hundred different jigsaw puzzles.

McIntyre was nuts to put him and Amy in charge of this "meeting." Ha! A global high-tech brawl was more like it — broadcast via private satellite to this chrome-and-silicon dome so Amy and Dan could be shouted down from all continents at the same time.

True, there had been some Cahill cooperation at the end of the Clue hunt. But it had come from the younger generation — Sinead and a handful of others. For example, Hamilton Holt was trying to keep his volatile father from going completely berserk. Ned, an Ekat like his sister, was providing useful information. And without Jonah's efforts, they could not hope to prevent Leila Wizard from bringing in the authorities.

Then there was Ian. It was impossible to set aside the awful fact that Ian's mother, Isabel Kabra, had set the fire that had killed Amy and Dan's parents. Ian and Natalie had been pretty much the Cahills' archenemies during the Clue hunt. In fact, you could depend on Ian to be a total bonehead about ninety-nine percent of the time. Now, however, seemed to be one of those rare moments when he could be depended upon to act as an ally, not an adversary. His sister was in danger, and he would do anything to aid in the rescue effort.

But if the younger generation was willing to find ways to work together, the older Cahills were as stubborn as mules.

"Why give this kidnapper what he wants?" Eisenhower demanded. "We can't let him get away with grabbing our people! That'll just encourage him to hit us again!"

"Dad, he's got Reagan!" his son argued.

"Hamilton's right," Amy put in quickly. "We're at Vesper One's mercy — at least until we can stage a rescue attempt. We have to figure out where he's h-holding the h-h-hostages —"

She's stammering like crazy now! Dan looked over to McIntyre, who was watching impassively as Amy floundered in front of the entire family.

Eisenhower's veins bulged as he waved off any effort from Hamilton to quiet him. "I'm not putting my daughter's life in the hands of a babbling teeny-bopper! You don't even know your own plan! Make up your mind! Are you kowtowing to this Vesper or are you looking for the hostages?"

That question — a specific inquiry about strategy — jolted Amy out of her helplessness. Maybe she lacked the nerve to shout down her squabbling relatives. But when it came to what needed to happen *now*, she knew exactly how to respond.

"We're going to do *both*!"

Her back straightened, and she peered directly into the camera that was broadcasting her around the world. "I propose a two-pronged response," she continued, her stammer gone. "Dan and I will travel to Italy to follow Vesper One's demands. We have no choice. The safety of our hostages depends on that. Meanwhile, Sinead will set up a Cahill command center right here in Grace's house. Ian, will you help her?"

"I'll be on the next flight," Ian promised.

"The command center will have two missions. First, to figure out where the hostages are being held so we can rescue them. Second, we have to answer the biggest question of all: Who are the Vespers and what do they want? They've been dogging our family for centuries, yet they're a total question mark. As horrible as these kidnappings are, they could be just the beginning. If we're at war, we'd better learn something about our enemies. Especially since they seem to know an awful lot about us."

Dan watched in amazement as his sister secured promises of cooperation from Cahills in every corner of the globe.

She used to hate public speaking, he marveled. *She still hates public speaking.*

Yet here she was, persuading the unpersuadable. She was almost scary—and somehow weirdly familiar.

It came to him in an instant. She reminded him of Grace, their enigmatic grandmother — aviator, explorer, adventurer, and Clue hunter extraordinaire — the most influential Cahill since Gideon himself. The resemblance came not so much in Amy's appearance as in her posture — ramrod straight, bent slightly forward, as if leaning into the next challenge. And there was no mistaking their grandmother's unwavering singleness of purpose. It was a shock to see it emanating from his sister.

"So it's settled, then," Amy concluded, her voice and image beaming around the world to dozens of computers, screens, and smartphones. "Dan and I will be on the ground in Italy, keeping Vesper One happy. But Sinead and Ian will keep you posted from here. Wish us luck."

Ian interrupted from monitor 4. "Is that the cat?" Saladin was marching across keyboards, tail in the air. "That cat hates me."

"Why should it be different from everybody else, Lucian?" growled Eisenhower.

McIntyre appeared at Amy's elbow. "That's exactly the kind of infighting that could get our loved ones killed," he warned. "We are more than merely Lucian, Janus, Ekaterina, Tomas, and Madrigal. We are all Cahills, and we are under attack."

Amy cut the connection.

She sighed tremulously. "Well, I did my best. I don't know if any of them believed me."

McIntyre placed a gentle hand on her slender shoulder. "You did wonderfully well, my dear. You cannot expect to erase five hundred years of mistrust and animosity in a ten-minute conversation. I don't think anyone could have done better — and I include your grandmother in that."

When the ringtone sounded, four sets of eyes flashed to the strange Vesper phone in Dan's hand. But it was dark and silent.

"Oh, it's mine." Amy glanced at her own cell but made no move to answer it. "It's Evan."

"Aren't you going to pick up?" asked Sinead after the third ring.

Amy shook her head. "He knows nothing about the Cahill side of my life, and I intend to keep it that way. I don't want to lie to him. . . ." She fell silent, looking torn.

"Don't you think the guy's going to notice when you disappear off the face of the earth?" Dan put in. "You see each other every day, and the rest of the time you're on the phone with him. When you don't show up at school, he's going to call the cops."

Amy flushed. "You know, it's hard enough to keep a relationship going without your entire family putting their two cents in!"

"Poor you," Dan shot back. "I'm sure the hostages' hearts are bleeding over your love life."

Amy relented. "I'll text him," she promised. "After we pack."

CHAPTER 4

The taxi sat stalled in traffic on London's M4, en route to Heathrow Airport.

Ian Kabra stewed in the backseat — and not entirely because his sister had been kidnapped and he was in danger of missing his flight. Oh, how he longed for the fleet of chauffeured Bentleys his family still maintained. That kind of luxury was not for him and Natalie anymore. They were poor now — better get used to it. Their mother had disowned them, and they had only four million American dollars to their name, which translated to less than three million pounds. Chicken feed.

If Ian didn't take to poverty, Natalie liked it even less. Her whole life was shopping and luxury and comfort. Their reduced circumstances were probably more of a bother to Natalie than the fact that she was being held hostage.

He felt a pang. She was his little sister and she was in danger. Wherever she was right now, it wasn't the back of a chauffeur-driven Bentley, either.

Once, in the Lucian stronghold in Paris, Ian's father had shown him a Tomas who had been abducted for questioning. Ian recalled a huge bear of a man — someone who should have feared nothing and nobody. Yet when Ian had looked through the one-way glass, he'd seen raw terror in those large bloodshot eyes.

Now it made perfect sense. How else would it feel to be in the hands of enemies, dependent on their mercy for your very life?

If the Tomas had cracked under the pressure, what chance did poor Natalie stand? How scared she must feel. How alone.

Ian felt pretty alone himself — about to cross an ocean to the company of former adversaries who were not quite friends.

And their cat.

Only for Natalie. It was funny. He didn't even like Natalie. Not *really*. But now that Mum had disowned them and Father was out of the picture, Natalie was his whole family.

He regarded the cell phone in his hand. It didn't have to be that way; it *shouldn't* be that way. There should be people to care when something bad happens to you.

His index finger trembled as he punched in the number he had not dialed in more than two years.

"Well, look who finally remembered that he has a mother!" came the voice on the other end of the line.

"How are you, Mum?"

"You don't care how I am. What's the purpose of this call?"

Ian swallowed hard. "There's bad news, Mum. Natalie's been kidnapped."

There was a pause—one of shock? Alarm? Worry? And then Isabel Kabra's cold voice spoke again: "And I should care about this because . . . ?"

"Because she's your daughter!" Ian exploded.

"Daughter? I *had* two children, but they both betrayed me. I confess it was difficult at first. But the reward is that now I don't have to think about either of them."

"You're a powerful woman! You could help her!"

"AidWorksWonders is my life now. If I become involved in anything other than that, it's a parole violation. I'm not going back to prison for the sake of a daughter I no longer have."

"Very well, you hate us now," Ian pleaded. "But you loved us once. We were a real family—"

"Oh, dear, you must be going under a bridge. What a poor connection!"

Click.

To Ian's utter humiliation, he found himself in tears.

The driver passed back a tissue. "That's some mother you got there, mate."

"She's under a lot of stress," Ian explained, wondering why he'd bother to defend such a terrible woman.

Amy and Dan loaded their small suitcases and backpacks into McIntyre's Lincoln for the ride to Logan Airport.

Amy hugged Sinead, and Dan scratched Saladin under the collar. "Later, Saladin. Take it easy on Kabra. On second thought, don't."

"You two have to promise to be careful!" Sinead handed Amy a small plastic bag. "I made you a going-away present — a high-powered miniature smoke bomb. Could come in handy against the Vespers. It works with knockout gas, so I tossed in a couple of breathing filters."

"That's the Cahill equivalent of a Hallmark moment," Dan observed. "A smoke bomb. When you care enough to send the very best — explosives."

"I'm not a flowers-and-candy kind of girl," Sinead informed him.

Amy smiled warmly. "It's sweet. Only — how are we going to get it through airport security?"

"It'll appear as a lollipop on the X-ray," Sinead explained. "Just don't break off the stick. That's the detonator."

McIntyre started the car and rolled down the window. "You've got a plane to catch."

Amy took the shotgun seat, Dan climbed into the back, and they started down the driveway. Although Amy had spent most of the last two years preparing for this moment, it was hard to wrap her mind around the reality that it was starting again.

She caught a glimpse of her brother in the side mirror. His face was expressionless, his eyes distant. He was gone again, visiting himself inside his own head. It had been like that ever since the end of the Clue hunt. He'd become such a loner. He had no friends, really—except for a strange boy named Atticus Rosenbloom. Dan had met him online. At only eleven, Atticus was two years younger. But Dan had assured Amy that his new friend was, in actuality, a total genius with a 200-plus IQ. Whatever that meant. The phrase "in actuality" came up around Atticus a lot. He was, in actuality, mature for his age. He'd also (in actuality) lost his mother, which was a pretty big thing for him and Dan to have in common. He lived with his father and older half brother in Boston, forty miles away. They'd only met in person a couple of times.

Amy worried about Dan more and more often lately. What sister wouldn't, watching her brother sink into darkness and isolation? Like today—threatening to light three gasoline-soaked men on fire. True, the move had probably saved Amy and Dan from joining the ranks of the abductees. . . .

But what thirteen-year-old would even think of that?

And if the attackers hadn't fled, then what? Would he have lit that fire?

Her cell phone interrupted her troubled reflections. She realized instantly who it must be.

"You *still* haven't called him?" exclaimed Dan from the backseat. "If you were *my* girlfriend—"

"I'm not!" Amy interrupted savagely, fishing the handset out of her pocket.

The gate at the edge of the property swung open automatically, and the big Lincoln roared onto the road.

"Evan, I'm so sorry—"

The cry came from both inside the phone and outside the car. McIntyre slammed on the brakes. The Lincoln screeched to a halt perhaps half a foot from a terrified figure frozen like a deer in headlights.

Amy leaped out of the car. "Evan! Are you all right?"

Evan performed a quick pat-down on his body, as if confirming that everything was still attached. It was such a cartoon gesture that she smiled in spite of herself. How cute was this guy, even when he was being a geek? It only boosted her regret at having to lie to him.

"Why are you skulking outside my house?"

He was outraged. "I'm worried about you! You won't answer my calls!"

"I was just dialing you."

"Yeah," he agreed, "eight hours later. This morning you fight off terrorists like you're Jackie Chan, and then you disappear! What's going on?"

"We're on our way to the airport," Amy admitted. "It's kind of a family emergency."

He was mystified. "You don't *have* any family!"

"This is more like extended family," she explained hurriedly. "Look, I've got to go."

"When will you be back?"

"I don't know." She understood how lame it sounded, but there was really nothing else to say.

"Ames" — Evan's lip quivered for an instant — "if you're trying to break up with me, why don't you just come out with it?"

"I'm not!" she exclaimed in horror. She could see Dan in the back, smirking at her through the tinted window, enjoying her discomfort. When he wasn't lost in space, he could be as annoying as ever.

McIntyre tooted the horn.

She looked pleadingly at Evan. "One day I hope I can explain. . . ." It was all she could offer without lying.

"Yeah, but when?"

No fair, thought Amy. This was the guy she'd been working on since freshman year. And now — finally — everything was perfect. But there was a plane to catch and lives at stake. And Evan — awesome, wonderful Evan — had to fall to the bottom of the priority list.

"I'll call. This time I really will." She jumped in the passenger door, and they squealed off, leaving Evan in a cloud of exhaust.

"Don't think of it as losing a boyfriend," Dan snickered. "Think of it as gaining a stalker."

Amy slumped in her seat. "On top of everything else, I'm going to get dumped."

The car drove on. Next stop: Logan Airport, en route to Florence, Italy.

And then what?

CHAPTER 5

Nellie Gomez awoke to a splitting headache. Worse, she was still hungry.

"Where's my croissant?" she demanded of the person leaning over her.

"Dear child," came a strangely familiar voice.

"Don't 'dear child' me!" she snapped. The twenty-two-year-old punk rocker ran black-polished fingernails through black-and-orange-dyed hair, which did nothing to soothe the pounding behind her black-shaded eyes. "Give me my croissant or I'll—"

It was then that she realized she was threatening the venerable Alistair Oh. "Alistair, what are you doing here?"

"The same thing we all are, I fear," came the reply. "We've been kidnapped."

That banished the headache. Nellie sat bolt upright and looked around. Fiske Cahill, Reagan Holt, and Natalie Kabra flanked Alistair. Ted Starling sat on a straight-backed wooden chair, staring at nothing with sightless eyes. All five wore baggy jumpsuits.

"Where are we?" Nellie demanded. "What *is* this place?" She examined her surroundings. Sterile white walls; no windows; high air vents, well out of reach; cameras everywhere.

"We were hoping you would know," Fiske sighed. "Underground, perhaps. Or in some kind of bunker. We don't see our jailers. Food comes in through that dumbwaiter in the corner."

"Has anybody seen Amy and Dan?" *Oh, God, please don't let them be part of this. . . .*

Fiske read her mind. "Thankfully, they seem to have escaped our fate."

"So far," Nellie agreed grimly. She got up and began to prowl around. The main area was surrounded by small bedrooms containing bunk beds. It wasn't luxury, but it wasn't a dungeon, either.

She walked over and banged on the dumbwaiter. *"Hey! I want to talk to the guy in charge!"*

"I already tried that," Reagan told her. "You never get an answer. All you get is a sore throat." She was as restless as a jungle cat. Lack of physical activity made all the Holts that way.

"I believe we're in the United States somewhere," Fiske offered. "Or possibly Mexico."

"How do you figure that?" asked Nellie.

"I was in California," he replied. "And since I arrived here first, that might indicate that my travel time was the shortest."

"I was second," put in Reagan. "Puerto Rico."

"Harrods," Natalie added wanly. "The new collections had just come in."

"The boys and I were in Tel Aviv," Alistair added. "Ned got away, I hope."

"Or they killed him," Ted said quietly.

"And I was in Paris," Nellie concluded. "I think I'm missing the soufflé test at the Académie." She looked at her watch, only to find it gone.

"No watches, no cell phones," Fiske supplied. "Our captors don't want us to know what time it is, or even what day."

"And they have a ghastly sense of style," Natalie mourned, gesturing toward a rack of jumpsuits in varying sizes. "I hope someone pays the ransom soon."

"If it's ransom they're after," added Ted.

"What else could it possibly be?" demanded Natalie, a shrill edge to her voice.

Nellie thought she might know. Synchronized kidnappings from different places around the world. An organized, coordinated operation, all the victims Cahills. Her eyes met Fiske's.

A buzzer went off inside the suite. It was so loud that all six captives grabbed at their ears and winced in pain. The main door whisked open and a new arrival was deposited on the floor.

Reagan flung herself at the opening, but she was a split second too late. The panel slid shut, leaving an unbroken wall. She bounced off, shouting and nursing her shoulder.

The buzzer ceased, and blessed quiet descended.

Nellie rushed over and knelt beside the new arrival. "He's just a kid!"

Natalie frowned. "Who is he? I thought they were only kidnapping Cahills."

"A case of mistaken identity, perhaps?" Alistair mused.

"I don't think so." Reagan pointed to the clothing rack. On one end hung a child-size jumpsuit. "They were expecting him."

With a groan, the boy rolled over and sat up, revealing his face in full.

"He *is* a Cahill," said Fiske in recognition. "Meet Phoenix Wizard, Jonah's young cousin."

The boy began to blink, and Nellie put her arms around him. He reminded her of Dan back when she was first hired on as the Cahill kids' au pair. "Phoenix — you okay, kiddo?"

"I — I don't know." He surveyed the suite. "Where am I?"

"You're with family," Nellie replied. It was the most comforting thing she could think of in a situation that was far from comforting.

Amy and Dan flew first class to Florence — sleeper seats, great food, attentive service.

It was still boring.

It all came back to Dan. During the Clue hunt,

they'd crisscrossed the globe on everything from experimental helicopters to yak-drawn carts. It was the same old story — long trips, nothing to do but twiddle your thumbs while your butt falls asleep. Right now Dan's butt was in such a deep slumber that it felt as if it had slipped into a coma.

"I hate this!" he mumbled aloud, hoping that Amy would wake up so he could fight with her just to pass the time.

No such luck. Amy was out like a light. She'd become pretty good at that. She was usually a nervous wreck, but she'd developed the ability to power nap, so when it was time for action, she'd be rested and ready. It was part of the new Amy — along with martial arts, rock climbing, calisthenics with Sinead, and the comm. center in the attic. *Be prepared* — wasn't that the Boy Scout motto? Well, she had been.

Not that all the preparation in the world would have stopped those seven kidnappings.

Dan couldn't get over the sense that they might be overlooking a much simpler solution. The Clue hunt was history, the serum destroyed, along with the list of ingredients. But there was one copy of the recipe that could never be eliminated. Dan had a photographic memory that was one hundred percent reliable. He couldn't forget the formula no matter how hard he tried. It was imprinted on his engrams.

If I'm stuck with the blueprint for Gideon's freak juice in my head, I should at least get some use out of it!

Why not whip up a batch, bang it down with a root beer chaser, and pound the Vespers into hamburger? Problem solved.

Amy would never let him do it. She was convinced the serum was bad news. Gideon's discovery had touched off five centuries of backstabbing, sabotage, and murder. Actually *taking* the formula, she had argued many times, would be just too dangerous and unpredictable.

But if things got really terrible, shouldn't they at least consider it? Who could predict what the Vespers were really up to? Some things, he thought grimly, were worse than five hundred years of treachery and feuding.

He might have slept, or perhaps dozed off and on. But before he could get any real rest, the captain restored the cabin lights and announced that they were about to land in Zurich, Switzerland. From there, it would be a short hop on a commuter flight to Peretola Airport near Florence.

They were on the ground in the transit lounge when the electronic chime sent Amy scrambling through her backpack for the special Vesper phone. She stared at the screen for a moment and then handed it to Dan.

It showed a photograph of a stark white, featureless room. There, wearing prison-style jumpsuits, were the seven Cahill hostages. The picture was captioned by only two words:

CAM 4: OUR GUESTS

"Send it to the comm. center," Amy quavered. "Sinead can blow it up, analyze it."

"That's all it is to you?" Dan exploded. "Something to be analyzed? That's Nellie! And Fiske! Even Alistair, the old goofball."

"We don't help them by falling to pieces," Amy reasoned. "We help them by figuring out where they are. Maybe something in the picture will tell us that."

Dan forwarded the picture to his laptop and then established the link to upload it to the comm. center in Grace's house. When he looked away from the screen, he saw that his sister was holding a Ziploc baggie containing a small spiral notebook.

"What's that?"

"McIntyre gave it to me while you were packing," Amy told him. "It was one of the only things that survived the fire that destroyed Grace's original house."

She removed the notebook from the plastic bag and handed it to Dan. It was seared and blackened, but a little bit of their grandmother's handwriting remained.

He felt a twinge of emotion. More than two years had passed since Grace's death. To behold something that was uniquely hers made the loss feel fresh again. He could see his sister blinking rapidly and knew she was having the same reaction.

"I can't understand a word of it," Amy went on in fond exasperation. "It's classic Grace—her own weird shorthand, practically code. McIntyre says it's mostly clue hunt stuff. But there are several entries marked with the letters VSP that might be about the Vespers."

Dan looked at her, eyes alight. "You think Grace knew things about them that she didn't tell the other Cahills? Not even her fellow Madrigals?"

Amy shrugged. "It wouldn't be the first time."

Dan flipped through the pad and found the clearest page.

VSP 79 – PUNY DESCRIBED FIRST TEST

He frowned. "'Puny'?"

"I saw that, too," Amy confirmed. "McIntyre has no idea what it means."

"If there's a Vesper One, there might be a Vesper Seventy-nine," Dan suggested. "And he's a really short guy."

"The Vespers are run by a Council of Six," his sister reminded him. "Vesper One could be the top spot on the council—followed by Vesper Two, and so on down to Six. They've probably got hundreds of agents, maybe thousands. But I doubt they're numbered beyond the council."

"Yeah, I figured it couldn't be that easy," Dan grumbled.

The computer beeped as the upload completed. A moment later, Ian Kabra appeared on the screen.

Dan was surprised. "Hey, Ian, isn't it, like, two in the morning back there?"

"It's called jet lag," Ian informed him. "I'm still on London time. I don't suppose you savages have any tea in this mausoleum."

"There's diet Snapple in the fridge."

Ian shuddered. "I thought not." He removed the picture from the printer and smiled grimly. "Poor Natalie. She won't like that jumpsuit."

Amy peered over Dan's shoulder. "Thanks for getting there so fast. Hey, what happened to your face?"

Dan instantly recognized the angry scratch that stretched from the corner of Ian's eye all the way along the olive skin of his cheek to his chin. "Have you been messing with Saladin?"

"No. Saladin has been messing with me," Ian shot back.

"He isn't big on Lucians," Dan explained. "Animals are really good judges of character."

"Spare me." Ian glowered at him. "Any word on what your 'task' is going to be?"

Dan shook his head impatiently. "I hate this waiting. Why can't Vesper One just come out and tell us?"

"He's keeping you off balance," Ian reasoned. "It's sound strategy. Everything he's done so far shows a mastery of the tactical arts."

Dan regarded his cousin on the laptop. Lucians were masters of cunning and calculation. They had been absolutely ruthless during the Clue hunt.

All that was in the past, of course.

So why was Ian saying nice things about Vesper One?

CHAPTER 6

Florence. The Jewel of the Renaissance.

"This place could really use a facelift," Dan commented as the taxi bore them past churches, palaces, monasteries, art galleries, and public gardens.

"You're kidding, right?" Amy was literally buried in reports. File folders containing every scrap of Cahill knowledge on the country of Italy were piled in her lap or on the seat beside her. She fumbled to unfold a huge road map. "Florence is the one truly preserved Renaissance city left. It's a UNESCO World Heritage Site."

"Yeah, but why does everything have to be so *old*?" Dan complained.

She glared at him with the impatience of the frazzled. "We don't have time for this."

"Yes, we do. Until we get the next message from Vesper One, we've got nothing to do at all." His stomach gurgled loudly. "I'm starving. When we check in to our hotel, let's ask the desk clerk where we can find one of those vast pizzas."

"What are you talking about?"

"Your guidebook says Florence is a city of vast pizzas. Look it up yourself."

"Those are vast *piazzas*, not pizzas! It means public squares!"

Dan's face fell. "Oh."

Amy sighed. "I honestly thought the clue hunt took the dweeb out of you. No such luck."

The text from Vesper One came in as they were settling into their suite at the Hotel Ilario.

```
Welcome to Florence.

You now know that our guests are well
treated. So far.

Your task: In the Uffizi Gallery, there
is a painting by Caravaggio called
"Medusa." You will steal it and await
instructions.

The consequences of failure will be
the same. One Cahill will die. You've
seen the photograph. Eeny meeny.

Vesper One
```

"A *painting*?" Dan was bewildered. "*That's* what he wants? I kind of thought he was going to make us give him your watch. Wasn't that what the Vespers were after last time?"

Amy was white as a sheet. "Not just a painting," she breathed. "A Caravaggio—a national treasure. No, a masterpiece like that belongs to *everybody*."

"Don't I wish," Dan put in. "If it was part ours we could just go to that gallery place and say, 'Can we borrow our Garbaggio for a couple of days?'"

"Caravaggio," Amy corrected. She was so distraught by the task ahead that she wasn't even annoyed at Dan's butchery of the painter's name. "His work inspired Rubens, Bernini, Rembrandt, and dozens of others! We'll be committing a crime against all countries and all people!"

"Is it even possible?" Dan wondered. "You've been in enough museums to know they've got security up the wazoo! You can't just pull a painting off the wall and stick it in your back pocket."

"It doesn't matter," she told him. "He's got our people. He's got Nellie. We have to find a way to give him what he wants."

"How?"

"First things first," Amy decided. "Let's go look at some art."

The Uffizi Gallery, on the banks of the river Arno, was housed in a building that was begun in the sixteenth century. The long U-shaped structure was originally a mammoth office complex — the word *uffizi* meant *offices* in Italian. To stand in its narrow central courtyard, gazing up at the two mammoth wings, was an instant transformation back to Medici times. In those days, great artists like Da Vinci and Michelangelo had used the Uffizi for both work and recreation. By the mid-eighteenth century, it had become a full-fledged art museum, open to the public. Today it housed — bar none — the greatest collection of medieval and Renaissance art anywhere.

Dan was not impressed by art galleries, and the Uffizi was no exception. "Fat naked babies. Big deal."

Amy heaved an exasperated sigh. "They're cherubs and angels."

She had always dreamed of visiting this place of so much fabled beauty, but today she saw none of it. The only thing that attracted her attention was the security — guards, locks, wires, cameras, pressure plates, alarm Klaxons. And those were just the visible features. Hard experience had taught her that the biggest danger often lay in those factors that could not be prepared for.

Another concern was the crowd. The museum was one of the most popular tourist attractions in Italy. Visitors seemed to be everywhere. Even if two would-be art thieves could manage to elude the Uffizi's vaunted security, they would never be alone with the object of their plan. At best, they would have to commit the crime in front of fifty witnesses.

"All right, where's the 'Medusa'?" asked Dan.

A gallery map directed them to the third floor — the Caravaggio room.

They saw it instantly. It was impossible to overlook, and not just because it was one of the few pieces that was not religious in nature. It was somewhat smaller than most of the works in the room — a round canvas mounted on a wooden shield about two feet in diameter.

"Whoa —" breathed Dan.

Amy followed up with "Ewww."

The image on the shield was the severed head of Medusa, her snake hair wild and unruly, blood still running from her neck. The eyes were wide and staring, the expression a perfect mask of horror, hatred, and ugliness. It looked so real and had so much depth that it was like a disembodied head coming at you with evil intent.

They were silent for a while, just staring, too mesmerized to look away.

Dan found his voice first. "If this is Vesper One's favorite painting, then it says an awful lot about the guy."

"We don't have to love it," Amy whispered. "We just have to steal it."

They pushed through the crowd to get a closer look. The shield was mounted on the wall rather than hung like a regular piece. It had a narrow metal frame. It didn't seem very heavy, but of course, they wouldn't know that until they were lifting it.

If they ever got that far.

There were two uniformed watchmen in the Caravaggio room as well as two security cameras. Amy scanned the space for blind spots. Between the guards and the video surveillance, there were none. The only possible cover was human — hiding in the midst of a crowd.

But crowds are made up of people, and people are unpredictable.

An art class arrived — a teacher with a dozen or so students carrying portfolios. They established themselves on various benches and began to sketch.

Dan sidled over to one of the watchmen. "Pretty packed today."

"It is always, as you say, packed," the guard replied proudly. "The Uffizi attracts nearly two million visitors each year."

"Sweet," Dan acknowledged. "Were you work-ing here a few years back when they had that big art heist?"

The man bristled. "There has never been a robbery at the Uffizi in modern times."

Dan looked surprised. "Are you sure? I heard some guy snatched one of those naked baby paintings, stuck it under his coat, and walked right out the door with it."

The guard laughed. "This is impossible. At the Uffizi? Never. Each artwork has its own weight sensor. If a piece is removed, an alarm sounds, and every entrance locks down automatically. Your thief would never get out."

Dan swallowed the rising lump in his throat. "I must have been thinking of some other museum. Maybe yours was the night robbery. They broke in through the roof and—"

Now the man was truly amused. "What imagi-nations you Americans have! At night the Uffizi is a fortress. Where there are no guards there are motion sensors. Not even a little moth could get in."

"Sweet," Dan said with very little enthusiasm.

They remained in the Caravaggio room a few more minutes and then explored possible exits from the museum via elevator or stairs. There seemed to be no quick way out before an alarm would trigger a lockdown.

When they examined the door that provided access

to the rooftop sculpture garden, Amy spotted small wires. So escaping up rather than down was not an option, either. This entrance was undoubtedly linked to the security system.

Once outside, they strolled through the long central courtyard, stepping past the Doric screen to the Arno.

"You know," Dan said in annoyance, "if I owned a hideous piece of 'art' like the 'Medusa,' I wouldn't turn my museum into Fort Knox with every high-tech gizmo money can buy. I'd be praying for some art thief to bust in and take it off my hands."

Amy drew in a breath. "It's not going to be easy." The task that lay ahead was so overwhelming that she couldn't quite wrap her mind around it.

Don't even try, she advised herself. *Break the whole operation down to individual problems. Solve one at a time. . . .*

"You mean you think there's a way to get in there and get out again with Miss Congeniality under your arm?" Dan demanded.

"There's always a way," his sister lectured. "We'll need help, though."

"What help?"

Amy grinned. "Sometimes it doesn't hurt to be part of the most powerful family in human history."

CHAPTER 7

The landing wheels kissed the tarmac, and the Gulfstream G6 taxied along the runway of Florence's small Peretola Airport. Behind a row of riot police, hundreds of young Tuscan girls screamed, cheered, and threw flowers.

The door of the jet opened, and the star himself appeared, ramping up the excitement level.

"Wassup, yo?" greeted Jonah Wizard.

The throng went berserk for ten solid minutes, while Jonah pretended to be surprised and overwhelmed by such a reception—as if it didn't happen everywhere he went.

Camera flashes exploded, and a babble of questions rose from the assembled reporters and paparazzi.

"Jonah, is it true that *Gangsta Kronikles* is being rereleased in 3-D?"

"What about the rumor that you're training to be a cosmonaut on a Russian space mission?"

"Why have you lost touch with your mother, Cora Wizard, the sculptor?"

"Jonah, what's the reason for your trip to Florence?"

"Since when does there have to be a reason?" Jonah replied airily. "Florence is off the chain! I'm just here to kick it with some homeys and soak up a little culture."

Toward the rear of the crowd, Amy and Dan paid no attention to their famous cousin and his usual hip patter. Their eyes were on Jonah's entourage, who were unloading the star's luggage from the G6's cargo bay. More specifically, they watched a muscular young man handling an unwieldy parcel that was carefully wrapped and secured.

While the shrieking crowd surged to follow Jonah's progress to the terminal, Amy and Dan intercepted the burly member of Jonah's posse.

"You got it?" Dan hissed.

The young man turned and raised the flat visor of his *Wiz-Up Tour 2010* baseball cap to reveal the grinning features of Hamilton Holt. "Hey, guys. How's it going?"

"How *should* it be going?" Amy asked wearily.

Hamilton turned serious. "Any word on Reagan?"

"We saw a picture," Amy informed him. "They all look okay, but you've got to figure they're pretty shaken up."

"Let's check out the merchandise," Dan prodded.

"Not here," Hamilton warned. "There's a VIP suite in the terminal. Jonah's meeting us there."

"Check it out."

Jonah removed the bubble wrap and held up the picture for his three cousins.

Dan took a step backward. The shock was almost as powerful as it had been the day before at the Uffizi. "It's perfect! It's every bit as disgusting as the real one!"

Amy nodded. "And so fast. We only called you yesterday."

Jonah shrugged. "Even the Janus take a short cut every now and then. You can do a lot with digitization these days. You break the picture down to squares and reproduce them one at a time. The other two are just as fly."

"You mean, just as hog ugly," Hamilton amended.

"The serpents don't help," Dan put in critically. "Live fat spaghetti. Look—that snake's biting the body of another one. Lady, if you're thinking of a modeling career, forget it!"

The rapper clucked sympathetically. "You guys just don't appreciate the power of the visual image. The Wiz used to be like that—until *Gangsta Kronikles*. When you're in the film industry, you understand the whole picture's-worth-a-thousand-words deal."

Hamilton rolled his eyes. "Here we go again."

Jonah picked up one of the "Medusa" copies. "Just look at this sucker. It's every slasher flick ever made packed into a single stomach-turning moment. That's why the Janus always respected Caravaggio. Back in the day, we tried to marry him into the family — Rembrandt's aunt, I think. He didn't go for it."

"If she posed for this picture, I can see why," Dan agreed.

"That wasn't it," Jonah told him. "The Janus records say Caravaggio was part of something bigger than the Cahills. Remember, the family was pretty new back then — only a few generations past Gideon's time. But I think the real reason artists love the 'Medusa' is the whole Da Vinci connection."

"*Leonardo* Da Vinci?" asked Amy, overawed.

"The story goes that somebody gave Da Vinci a shield to decorate, and he painted the face of Medusa on it — you know, turn your enemies to stone." A flash of the world-famous grin. "Nobody's ever seen Da Vinci's shield, but according to legend, Caravaggio used it as a model for his own 'Medusa.'"

Hamilton frowned. "How many 'Medusas' are there?"

"Only one 'Medusa' that matters," Amy told him with certainty. "The one we have to steal from the Uffizi."

Dan took a piece of paper from his pocket, unfolded it, and held it out in front of Jonah and Hamilton. "Here's some more stuff we're going to need."

1 pair coveralls
1 extension ladder (30 foot)
1 glass cutter
1 artist's portfolio (large)

1 water pistol

1 bottle india ink

1 portable trampoline (collapsible)

1 bicycle w/ basket

4 pizza boxes

Jonah whistled. "I hope you've got some crazy evil-genius strategy, 'cause—straight up—I don't get it."

Amy favored him with a slight smile. "You'll see."

CHAPTER 8

The next morning was chilly and clear. The streets of central Florence bustled with commuters on their way to jobs. Tourists moved at a slower pace, getting an early start on a day of sightseeing.

The Uffizi Gallery didn't open until eight-fifteen, so the famous building was deserted, except for a lone workman in coveralls, perched atop a ladder, polishing a high window. A sign at the base declared CAUTION in several different languages. A casual observer would never have noticed that the washer's interest extended only to one window — on the third floor, the Caravaggio room, number 43.

Hamilton Holt peered through the glass into the gallery. It wasn't hard to spot the "Medusa" on the far wall. God bless America, the real thing was even more hideous than Jonah's copies! Why anybody would want a train wreck like that was beyond Hamilton. Then again, the Holt family had never been big art fans. Ultimate fighting and tractor pulls were more their speed.

He took note of the mounted security cameras. Luckily, they were focused on the paintings, not the windows. From the pocket of his coveralls he took out the glass cutter and pressed it to the lower part of the frame, feeling the blade digging into the thick pane.

A uniformed figure stepped into the Caravaggio room. A security guard! Frantically, Hamilton hid the cutter behind his cloth and resumed his polishing. The man's eyes panned the various artworks on display and then settled on Hamilton outside the window.

A moment of fear. The Cahill team knew nothing of the window washing procedures at the Uffizi. Maybe the regular service used a crane or scaffolding. Maybe their uniforms were a different color. Maybe the Uffizi guards would recognize the usual employees.

The danger passed. The guard completed his sweep of the room and moved on.

Trembling with relief, Hamilton pocketed the cloth and wielded the glass cutter again.

Twenty-seven inches wide by four high, he said to himself.

Those had been Amy's instructions. Big enough to get the job done, but not so large — they hoped — that it would be noticed in the time between now and the heist, at eleven A.M.

He drew the blade across the glass, estimating the length of the incision. He removed the long rectangular strip of glass to ensure the cut had gone all the way through. Delicately, he replaced the piece, careful not

THE 39 CLUES

76

to push too hard. Broken window shards on the Uffizi floor would be a dead giveaway.

Dead . . .

The word resonated in his mind like a weight slamming against the stack of a Universal machine. If this robbery was a bust, Reagan and the other hostages might very well end up dead. The thought was a sucker punch to his gut, and he stumbled as he climbed down to street level and folded the ladder.

Hamilton thought the plan was crazy, but you didn't bring in a Tomas to think. Even as he aced his SATs and early acceptances rolled in from colleges everywhere, he understood that muscle would be his main role in the heist. He knew he was smart, but his sister's life was an awful lot to bet against five hundred years of Tomas history.

So he was here for the heavy lifting, leaving the strategy up to the others. Amy, Dan, and Jonah had been over it a hundred times, and the answer was always the same: If they couldn't get the painting out via the door, and they couldn't get the painting out via the roof, that left only one possible exit.

Through the window.

Zero hour was set for eleven A.M. to give the Uffizi a chance to fill up. That turned out to be unnecessary. By ten o'clock, the place was a mob scene. The crowd was mostly tourists, but there were art students as well, carrying sketching equipment in large portfolios. Amy blended right in — and *her* portfolio contained a lot more than paper and pencils.

She toured the gallery, marveling at masterpieces by Giotto and other Renaissance painters — huge triptychs and frescoes that left her thankful the "Medusa" was a manageable size. At 10:45, she made her way up to the Caravaggio room, taking note of the faint lines that marked the location of the window slit. Hamilton was already in position in the group surrounding the "Medusa."

It all seemed completely casual, but the place where she set down her portfolio had been very carefully chosen — just beyond the scrutiny of the security cameras.

The countdown began. Amy took out a pad and pretended to sketch, mostly to keep her hands from shaking. She had risked her own life many times during the Clue hunt; today it was the lives of seven others that hung in the balance.

She caught a sideways glance from Hamilton, noting that he was pale, and his T-shirt was dark with perspiration. Nobody could sweat like a Holt.

10:59. She watched, strangely detached, as the second hand of the wall clock swept up to zero hour.

Now.

Amy pulled a water pistol from the portfolio and shot a stream of ink at the near surveillance camera, coating the lens. Without hesitation, she turned to the other and did the same, just as the clock struck eleven.

Hamilton leaped forward and wrenched the "Medusa" off the wall. An earsplitting Klaxon howled. Throughout the Uffizi, doors slammed shut and locked. At the main entrance, heavy steel sheeting descended, blocking any escape. Security officers scoured banks of video monitors, searching for the source of the alarm. An army of guards fanned out around the building.

In the Caravaggio room, the visitors were frantic, shouting and screaming, bumping into one another and the four walls. Amy yanked the three "Medusa" fakes out of the portfolio and tossed them into the frenzied crowd. The instant the last copy left her hand, Hamilton Frisbee'd the real "Medusa" over the sea of bobbing heads. Amy caught it and in a single motion slipped it into the precut slit in the window.

The glass strip popped out easily, but the opening was too narrow for the convex shape of the shield.

Leave it to a Holt to make the hole too small!

Summoning all her martial arts training, Amy delivered a powerful karate kick to the window. The glass shattered, and the "Medusa" was falling, leaving the three forgeries and utter chaos in its wake.

The wail of the alarm was Dan's call to action.

He had the trampoline unfolded in seconds and looked up to see the painting plummeting earthward, much closer to the gallery wall than he'd anticipated.

Yikes! He scrambled to push the contraption flush against the building, but one of the collapsible bars caught in the cobblestones. In desperation, he hefted the entire frame and dove forward, his mind awhirl with visions of a four-hundred-year-old masterpiece shattering on the street right before his eyes. When the shield hit the trampoline, the webbing stretched with the force of impact and flung the artwork up and out. Dan gathered the "Medusa" into his arms like an NFL receiver making a highlight-film catch.

He hit the stones hard, but his precious cargo was unscathed.

Touchdown, Cahill!

He could already hear police sirens over the wail of the Uffizi Klaxon. The hottest item on the planet was in his hands. He had to make it disappear *fast*!

He placed the stolen artwork inside a pizza box. It fit so perfectly that he couldn't help wondering if Caravaggio himself might have designed it that way — a pizza-size "Medusa."

He shut the lid and stuck the box one from the bottom of a stack of four, which he loaded into the basket of a rusty bicycle. Then he got on the bike — it was a little too big — and began a wobbly ride away from the gallery.

Police were streaming from every direction, surrounding the Uffizi. Dan pedaled faster, determined to put some distance between himself and the scene of the crime. He jounced along the uneven stones, turning toward the river. He could see the water straight ahead, but he could also see cops — lots of them — forming a makeshift roadblock.

No need to freak, he told himself. *You're just a regular pizza guy, doing your job.*

The officers were all around him now, stopping cars and pedestrians, jabbering in excited Italian. Any container larger than a wallet was searched. Dan set his eyes on the Arno, not daring to glance to the left or right as he rolled through the thick of the investigation.

The river was so close that he could read the names of the boats passing under the famous Ponte Vecchio. Just a few more yards! He was going to make it. . . .

"Fermati!" ordered a gruff voice.

A huge hand closed on his shoulder, bringing him and the bike to an immediate stop. A thick-necked policeman peered into Dan's face and then moved down to the flat boxes sitting in the basket. He flipped open the lid of the top one, revealing the sight and delectable aroma of a pizza margherita. Reaching below, he opened the second box. Parmesan and fresh basil.

With a grunt, he replaced both lids and waved Dan along. Grinning to conceal his relief, Dan pedaled on, truly amazed that he hadn't fainted and toppled into the gutter. If the officer had looked into the third pizza box, he would have found something not quite so appetizing — the face of the "Medusa."

He rode on shaky legs to the river's edge, veering

out of view of the roadblock he had just cleared. Right on schedule, a sleek powerboat appeared under the bridge. At the rail stood Jonah Wizard, holding a long-handled fishing net. The craft slowed as it approached the shore. Dan extracted the third pizza box from the stack and tossed it into the waiting net. Within a few seconds, the "Medusa" was drawn aboard, and the boat was back up to speed and gone.

The Uffizi Klaxon still howling in the background, Dan helped himself to a slice of pizza and sat down on the grass, sharing generously with the ducks on the Arno.

Art theft gave a guy an appetite.

CHAPTER 9

The Florentine police kept the Uffizi Gallery in full lockdown until the surveillance tapes could be scrutinized and every single visitor could be interrogated and searched. It was almost midnight by the time Amy and Hamilton were released by the authorities.

Once they were free and in a taxi back to their hotel, Amy called Dan, choosing her words carefully.

"Sorry to be so late. We got a little tied up at the museum. Terrible thing—a priceless painting has been stolen. How was your day?"

"Pretty good," Dan replied carefully. "Jonah and I shared a pizza at lunch."

"Got it," Amy acknowledged, flashing Hamilton a thumbs-up. "We'll be there soon."

Hamilton had a complaint. "Why did you have to tell the cops I'm your boyfriend? That's gross, Amy. We're related!"

Amy was disgusted. "We had a common ancestor, like, five hundred years ago. Besides, if they think we're together, we only have to come up with one story, and I can do all the talking."

"Hey, I got early acceptance at Notre Dame," Hamilton said defensively. "I can talk."

"Of course you can," Amy soothed. "It's what you say that might get us into trouble."

Back at the hotel, they walked into their suite, where an appalling sight met their eyes. There in the sitting room, glaring hideously down at them from the wall, was the "Medusa."

"Are you crazy?" Amy fumed. "What if room service sees it?"

Dan shrugged. "We don't need room service. We've got leftover pizza. Want a slice?"

Jonah peered critically up at the Renaissance masterpiece. "Man, the copies don't do it justice. This one's the truth!"

"Only a Janus," groaned Hamilton.

"Didn't anybody see you take it?" asked Dan.

Amy shrugged. "The cameras were blind, and the guards were going after the three fakes floating around the crowd. By the time they figured out anything was missing, we'd already slipped into the next room in the confusion."

Jonah regarded her with respect. "The Janus ought to put you on the payroll to scoop up a few of our artworks that fell into the wrong hands over the years."

A loud ringtone filled the parlor. Amy instinctively looked to the secure Vesper phone, but the sound was coming from her own cell phone, its vibrate function carrying it across the surface of the coffee table.

"Hello?"

Distant cheering wafted over the handset.

"I knew you could do it!" exclaimed Sinead's voice.

"Brilliant!" added Ian.

"Very well done," approved William McIntyre.

Amy smiled in spite of herself. In the awful tension of seven hostages in danger and the Vespers scheming toward who knew what terrible end, it was easy to overlook today's accomplishment. Stealing the "Medusa" was a despicable offense, not to mention a felony. But it was also an amazing achievement.

"How did you find out about it?" she asked.

"You made CNN," Sinead told her. "They're calling it the crime of the century."

"We're *not* criminals," Amy said defensively.

"You did what you had to do," McIntyre soothed. "Admirably. Now you just have to wait for instructions from Vesper One."

"How long will that take?" Amy wondered.

"Not long," Ian predicted. "If it made the news here, it stands to reason that it made the news where he is."

Their conversation was interrupted by a small commotion on the other end of the line. "What's going on?" Amy prompted.

She could hear urgent whispering in the background. Finally, Sinead hissed, "It's the police — they've arrested an intruder outside the main gate!"

A spark of alarm shot through Amy. "A Vesper?"

"Perhaps we can get a glimpse with one of the front security cameras," McIntyre suggested.

"I'm way ahead of you," Sinead confirmed. "Wait— I see him! Uh-oh—"

"What?" Amy demanded.

"It's Evan," Sinead told her with a sigh. "He's so sweet!"

Amy was aware of a mixture of relief and despair. Stubborn, loyal Evan. The very qualities that she admired most in him were coming back to haunt her.

"Who's Evan?" Ian asked.

"Amy's boyfriend!"

"Amy, since when do you have a boyfriend?" Ian probed.

"Since *none of your business*!" Amy exploded. "What's Evan doing at our gate? He knows I'm out of town."

"He is obviously trying to see if you're back *in* town," McIntyre explained patiently. "The young man truly cares for you. Since you won't respond to his calls, and your explanations have been woefully inadequate—"

"What do you want me to tell him?" Amy demanded. "The truth?"

"Certainly not," the lawyer replied, "but you might take the trouble to make your lies a little more convincing. There is an awkward stage at the beginning of any romance between Cahill and non-Cahill. When your mother and father first began courting, I clearly remember Hope explaining to Arthur—"

Sinead broke in. "The cops need to know what to do with Evan, Amy. What should I tell them?"

"Shoot to kill?" Ian suggested.

"That's not funny." Amy heaved a weary sigh. "Convince them to let him go. I'll call him and clear the air."

"You've said that before," Sinead reminded her.

"This time I mean it."

"I told you, Evan. It's a family emergency. I can't give you the details because it isn't all about me."

Evan's voice over the cellular network was rising with his dismay. "This is crazy, Ames! I was just arrested for *looking* at your house! Have you taken out a restraining order or something?"

"Of course not." Suddenly, the phone in her hand weighed sixty tons. It was hard enough dealing with the Cahill madness when you were part of it. But when the repercussions affected outsiders, it was almost too much to bear. "The police are keeping an eye on the place because of what happened on the bus. They think it might have been a kidnap attempt on me or Dan because of our inheritance from Grace." Oh, how she longed for the luxury of simply being honest with him. It would be easier for her, and it would save him so much anguish.

"Who's that new guy with the snooty accent who came out and talked to the police?" Evan persisted.

"He looks like some kind of male model."

"That's just my cousin Ian," Amy explained.

"Not much of a family resemblance," Evan noted sourly.

"He's like a twenty-fifth cousin, ten times removed."

Evan was not satisfied. "You won't tell me where you are. You won't tell me when you're coming back. You hardly answer my calls. You have to know how worried I am. If our roles were reversed, what would *you* do?"

"I — I —"

I will not stammer. Not with Evan, the one part of my life where I can just be me and my Cahill ancestry doesn't matter. . . .

"I'm sorry you feel so abandoned," she finished with effort. "I promise that will change. From now on —" The Vesper phone chimed, drawing all eyes in the hotel suite. "Gotta go," Amy babbled, and hung up on her boyfriend.

There was a footrace for the special smartphone. Hamilton got there first and held up the message for the others to see.

```
Very impressive. Remind me to go
shoplifting with you in happier times.
```

```
To business: Bring the merchandise to
the Medici crypt at the San Lorenzo
Basilica. Tomorrow, noon.
```

I hope your skill in acquiring this
item is matched by your punctuality in
handing it over. Tardiness will not be
tolerated.

Vesper One

"What about our hostages?" Hamilton yelled at the phone. "What about Reagan?"

"We can't text him back," Dan said grimly. "His location is blocked."

"Dude's asking a lot," Jonah observed. "How does he expect us to cough up the swag until he cuts loose our people?"

"He's got hostages," Hamilton reminded him. "We've got nothing."

The thought of Phoenix melted the expression of cocky defiance on Jonah's famous face. "If they hurt the little guy —"

Amy wished she had something encouraging to say, but they were at Vesper One's mercy.

And she was very much afraid that he had none.

CHAPTER 10

The Basilica of San Lorenzo was located in Florence's main market district. In the middle of the day, the narrow streets were crowded and progress was slow — especially for the long stretch limo provided by Jonah's Italian record company. With the car mired in traffic and the church's towering dome in view, the four Cahills abandoned their ride and ventured out on foot.

The "Medusa" was wrapped in a voluminous lawn bag in Amy's arms, but Dan was still nervous. All of Italy was looking for that thing — the whole world, really. Was it just his imagination, or were a lot of eyes turning their way? Maybe it was Jonah. Even with dark shades and the brim of his baseball cap pulled low, the famous face still seemed familiar.

The roar of powerful motors assailed Dan's ears. Six large Harley Davidsons were coming down the road, their black-jacketed riders weaving in and out of the creeping vehicles.

What motorcycle gang goes cruising in a traffic jam?

The thought had barely crossed his mind when the choppers were all around them. Before Dan's horrified eyes, the lead biker reached out and shoved Amy to the street. As she went down, a second rider wheeled around her opposite flank and wrenched the parcel from her arms.

"Hey!" Dan hurled himself at Amy's attacker, but in that instant, a third Harley blocked his way. A leather-clad stiff-arm shoved him back and he tumbled over the hood of a slow-moving taxi.

Two more motorcycles jumped the sidewalk, streaking past on the curbside. A boot kicked out, tripping Jonah from behind. Hamilton tried to fight back, but his punch slammed into a hard helmet. He shouted in agony, grasping swelling knuckles.

Amy was on her feet again, running full speed. The package was far ahead now, tracing a serpentine escape path through the snarl. A few seconds later, the gang disappeared around a corner. Dodging pedestrians and food carts, the four Cahills barreled after the rapidly fading engine noise.

Amy pounded around the corner and pulled up short. "Where'd they go?"

Dan plowed into her from behind and bounced off, gasping. "Keep running!"

"No use, cuz," wheezed Jonah, his shades lost, his famous eyes wild. "They're gone."

"No fair!" raged Hamilton. "Those guys ripped off what we rightfully stole!" He thought of what this might mean for Reagan, and his anger deflated to despair.

"Back to the limo!" Dan panted. "We'll search the whole city!"

Amy shook her head in resignation. "No."

"They've got the painting!" Dan raved. "It's the only thing we can trade for our people! For *Nellie*!"

"We'll never find them," Amy said desolately. "They're probably already in a basement somewhere, realizing they've got what every policeman in Italy is looking for."

There was a terrible silence as the gravity of the situation sank in. They had failed Vesper One. What would happen now? Their enemy had promised again and again to kill a hostage.

Who would it be? Alistair . . . Natalie . . . Ted . . . Phoenix . . .

Jonah winced as if in physical pain.

Reagan . . .

A tear pooled in the corner of Hamilton's eye.

Fiske . . . Nellie . . .

The Cahills' sibling radar had saved them so many times before, but at that moment, there was nothing to communicate but utter powerlessness and black, black despair.

When the Vesper phone chimed, they all jumped. Amy was trembling as she drew the device out of her pocket.

The small screen displayed two words:

"That's impossible!" Hamilton exclaimed. "How could the package be received when we never made the drop-off?"

Light dawned on Dan. "That *was* the drop-off! The Vespers didn't want to tell us where they'd be, so they set us up to get swarmed!"

"Slick," commented Jonah.

"Very slick," agreed Amy, rubbing a bruised hip. "Who *are* these Vespers?"

The abandoned gas station had been closed and shuttered for many years, but the service bay rattled open in perfect working order to admit the lone motorcyclist. The biker dismounted, pulling down the door behind him. He removed his helmet, and curly hair tumbled free.

Casper Wyoming had been named for the location of his parents' most successful bank heist. He had been born into crime and had also made it his life's passion. It was far more satisfying to steal a single dollar than to earn fifty by honest means. He had quickly risen through the ranks of the Vespers. Someday he intended to be Vesper One.

But until that day, the current Vesper One was expecting his report.

He reached into the green garbage bag and pulled out the shield-painting that the Cahill kids had stolen.

The image took his breath away. Such perfect ugliness! Caravaggio would have made an excellent Vesper. Few could match this artist's skill in creating pure horror.

Casper Wyoming had devoted his life to it.

What a shame that this magnificent artwork was too famous to sell! But of course its value to the Vespers went far beyond mere money.

He held the shield upright and turned the face away so that he was examining the backing. His spine stiffened, and he drew in a sharp breath. This was not the "Medusa"! This was a fake!

He was distracted by the clatter as the service bay door opened to admit a second motorcyclist, her helmet under her arm. The woman was young and blond, with slight features and a face that was very nearly angelic.

Casper held up the "Medusa" and then flipped the artwork around, revealing the back.

The newcomer's sweet smile slowly resolved itself into a diabolical grin. Treachery meant consequences. It was the Vesper way.

Someone was going to pay.

The mood inside the holding cell had gone from shock to fear to frustration, settling at last into a kind of resigned boredom. The determination to discover the nature of their captivity and to escape was as strong as ever. But they had made absolutely zero progress.

They did not know the identity of their captors. They did not know where they were being held. Ted insisted that he sometimes heard voices beyond the walls. The others believed him—his hearing seemed more acute due to his lack of sight. But so far, he had not been able to make out a single word, or even an accent.

At first, their plan had been to make a break for the door the instant the next hostage was delivered. But Phoenix had been the final arrival. Since he had been deposited on the floor, the walls of the cell had been their entire universe. Except for the dumbwaiter, which sent down meals and fresh laundry, they had no contact whatsoever with the outside world.

Yesterday, Reagan had climbed into the dumbwaiter, hoping to be hauled out as dirty dishes. She'd sat there for a solid hour before giving up. Their next meal had been a pitcher of water and a loaf of stale bread.

"Don't get me wrong—I hate these guys," was Nellie's opinion. "But when it comes to running a prison, they know what they're doing."

Fiske nodded sadly. "They have certainly put a great deal of effort into isolating us completely. We have been here several days and have learned nothing."

"Several days?" Natalie repeated. "I think I've missed my hair appointment."

"We've got bigger problems than your bad hair day," Nellie said irritably.

Reagan slammed her fist into her palm. "I can't stand it that we're just sitting around like helpless idiots!"

"It's very wearing," Alistair agreed, his right arm twitching. He felt incomplete without his walking stick. "Still, there's nothing for it but to wait until something happens. We can't act — we can only *react*. The next move belongs to our captors."

At that moment, the panel swept aside. Reagan did not hesitate. She ran headlong at the opening. The first thing she saw beyond the walls of their prison was a large hunting crossbow — the kind that could fell a buck at three hundred yards. It was pointed at a patch of skin between her eyes; range: eighteen inches. She backed away from the weapon and the masked jailer wielding it.

Another captor appeared behind the first, also masked. But instead of a bow, this one carried a small snub-nosed pistol. Holding it out in front of him, he approached the hostages.

Fiske stepped forward. "Put that thing away, and we can talk about this like civilized people." He was shoved aside and went sprawling into the rack of jumpsuits.

The jailer pointed the gun at the nearest captive — Natalie. The girl was so frightened that she could barely manage to shrink away from him.

"No."

The word resonated from all around them, as if the cell itself were a speaker. The hostages looked about in shocked bewilderment. The voice was electronically distorted, almost robotic sounding, yet the authority was unmistakable. The jailer with the pistol froze instantly, awaiting instructions.

"Not her," the voice boomed.

"Who, then?" he asked the four walls.

"Suit yourself."

It happened so quickly that no one had a chance to move defensively. With lightning speed, the jailer pointed the snub-nose at Nellie and squeezed the trigger. An earsplitting *crack* resounded in the small enclosed space.

Nellie clutched at her shoulder, her face twisted with pain. Dark red blood trickled out between her fingers. Before the horrified gaze of her fellow prisoners, she crumpled to the floor. Alistair rushed to her aid.

In a fury, Reagan flung herself at the attacker. Her action cost her dearly. The guard with the crossbow smashed the shaft of the weapon against the side of her head. She went down, stunned.

Both jailers backed out of the room. The wall swept shut behind then.

Phoenix and Natalie clung together, crying.

Ted stood up, helpless and bewildered. "What just happened?"

Fiske was closest to Reagan and hurried to help her up. "Very brave, my dear, but very foolish."

Alistair knelt beside Nellie and touched her neck, feeling for a pulse.

CHAPTER 11

The four cousins hadn't yet ordered a single item off La Rotunda's menu, yet their table was piled high with all the specialties of the house.

"Thanks, yo. 'Preciate that," the famous Jonah Wizard said graciously as the chef personally delivered a steaming platter of gnocchi.

"Signor Wizard!" the man gushed. "Such an honor to welcome a renowned television personality and recording artist!"

"And movie star," Jonah added helpfully. "Did you catch *Gangsta Kronikles* yet? Don't wait for the DVD."

"Of course, of course!" the chef exclaimed. "We will always remember this glorious day!"

"Me, too. Great chow." The visiting celebrity knew that this quote was going to appear in the next diners' guide, along with a new house specialty, probably called *Gangsta Gnocchi*.

They were tucked into a corner table to provide Jonah with a degree of privacy that he never got anyway. Patrons were constantly peering over at them, snapping pictures, and paparazzi hovered outside the big front window. It was a circus that the star was used to.

"Free food!" mumbled Hamilton, his mouth full. "No wonder you're rich. You don't have to pay for anything."

"Since when is it free?" Jonah demanded. "If I don't leave a crazy big tip, it'll be all over Europe that the Wiz is a cheapskate! They'll seat me behind the sound-man from the penguin movie at the Oscars!"

"Enough," said Amy impatiently. "Let's give a thought to what we're doing here."

With the heist complete, and the drop-off made, there was nothing left but to wait for the news that their hostages had been released. No one knew what form this would take. Would they receive a text from Vesper One directing them to a rendezvous point? Or would the call come from one or more of the seven, declaring themselves to be free? Would they still be together or scattered all around the world?

All cell phones were fully charged and on the table amid the plates of antipasto and osso buco. Halfway around the world in Massachusetts, Sinead, Ian, and McIntyre were in the comm. center, awaiting word. *Gideon*, the Cahill satellite, hung poised in orbit, ready to relay any and all information.

"What's taking so long?" Dan asked impatiently. "We gave them their ugly painting. All they have to do is open the door and let everybody out."

"They'll probably move them around," Amy reasoned. "You know—disorient them so they can't pinpoint where they were held, or the people who were holding them. That would take time."

"Eat something," Hamilton suggested, slurping pasta. "The steak rocks!"

"It's veal," Amy informed him.

When the chime sounded, the frenzy to grab at cell phones created what looked like a food fight at the table.

Amy snatched up the Vesper phone.

"What does it say?" Dan prodded. "Are they out?"

The four huddled together over the small screen.

```
Consequences. n.: The punitive payback
for an act of treachery or wrongdoing.

The painting is a fake. These are the
consequences:
```

Below the message, a short video began to play on the screen. It was the scene from the Vesper holding cell—Nellie's shooting.

Amy and Dan watched in horror as their former au pair went down in a heap.

"No—" Dan whispered.

"Oh, man," moaned Jonah, for once at a loss for something hip to say. "I'm really sorry, you guys. I'm totally down with how much she meant to you."

Hamilton nodded in silent agreement and looked away from the screen when his sister was bludgeoned with the crossbow.

Focus, Amy ordered herself. *Don't lose it.* But she could feel the tears coming. More, she could think of no reason why she should try to hold them back. She cried softly, and it took every ounce of her willpower not to scream her grief and outrage.

Don't cry, kiddo.

It was Nellie's voice that came to her, trying to soothe her. The effect was so real that she actually glanced up, almost certain that Nellie would be standing there in the restaurant, ready to take charge. How often had the au pair softened the blow for her and Dan over the years?

This time she had needed them, and they had failed her.

The voice was still there: *You worry too much, kiddo. Everything's fine.*

But nothing was fine. Nothing would ever be fine again. How were they going to live without Nellie?

She looked at Dan and could almost see him receding into that dark place he'd been visiting more and more lately.

"Why is it," he said faintly, "that sooner or later, everybody we love dies?"

Amy made no reply because she knew that if she opened her mouth the scream would still be there.

When they'd last seen Nellie, she'd been aglow with

the prospect of cooking school in Paris: *So long, you two. I hope I can trust you to stay out of trouble for a few weeks.*

The Cahills had actually been a little insulted.

Say your good-byes carefully, Amy now mourned. *You never know when it's your last chance.*

Hamilton's bark snapped her out of her reverie. "Wait!"

Amy came back to reality and focused on the smart-phone's monitor. The other hostages were gathered around Nellie in a state of excitement.

Dan inched closer. "Are her *eyelids* moving?"

Jonah was on his feet now, cheerleading. "Get up, babysitter! Up! Up!"

"Come on!" added Hamilton.

Amy crossed her fingers and toes and prayed.

The four watched as Reagan and Alistair slowly raised Nellie to a seated position. Her face was even paler than usual, her features contorted in agony. But she was clearly alive.

Amy let out a breath and realized for the first time she'd been holding it.

"Yeah!" shouted Jonah, twirling the much larger Hamilton around the restaurant in a victory dance.

The other diners looked on in amazement. This wild display was hardly the public image of too-cool-for-school Jonah Wizard.

"What's the matter?" Hamilton challenged. "Haven't you ever seen a happy rapper before?"

"Movie star," Jonah amended as the two cousins sat back down.

On the Vesper phone, the video ended, to be replaced by the words:

```
Still in the land of the living . . . so
far . . .
```

Dan bristled. "What's that supposed to mean?"

"It means they shot her in the shoulder to send a message," Amy reasoned in a shocked monotone. "The next bullet could be through her heart."

"Well, message received," Dan quavered. "I honestly thought—" His voice caught in his throat.

Amy reached over to touch his clenched hands. "Me, too."

"Can I say something?" ventured Hamilton, much subdued. "How could that painting be a fake?"

"Must have been insanity in the gallery," Jonah reasoned. "Any chance the real deal got swapped with one of the copies?"

"No way," said Amy firmly. "Hamilton threw it straight to me and I dropped it out the window. The 'Medusa' we gave them was the one from the wall."

"You think Vesper One lied about it, just to have an excuse to shoot a hostage?" Hamilton suggested.

"He never needed an excuse," Dan pointed out. "If all he wanted was blood, he could have murdered everybody on day one."

"Then there's only one explanation," Amy concluded. "If we handed over a fake, it's because that's what the Uffizi had hanging on their wall!"

"Yo, man, no fair!" Jonah complained. "They told us what to jack, and we went and jacked it! If it's the wrong thing, that's on them!"

Amy sighed. "Even if we could make Vesper One believe that, we have no way to get in touch with the guy."

"That's *his* problem!" Hamilton shot back. "We didn't ask for a one-way phone!"

"There's no such thing as his problem, only *our* problem," Amy explained wearily. "He holds our people, and he's just shown that he doesn't mind shooting hostages. If the 'Medusa' is a fake, we have to track down the real one."

"Are you serious, Amy?" Dan exploded. "That painting's hundreds of years old! It could be anywhere by now! For all we know, it burned in a fire or sank to the bottom of the ocean!"

Amy set her jaw. "In the clue hunt, we found things on mountaintops and in underwater cities. Why would you doubt we can find this?"

Hamilton was wide-eyed. "Yeah, but where would you even start to look?"

"This is a famous cultural treasure," Amy replied. "From the moment the paint dried, people were talking about it, writing about it, cataloging it." She stood up. "We start looking in the library."

CHAPTER 12

Nellie lay on her bunk in the Vesper holding cell, propped up by pillows donated by the other six hostages.

Young Phoenix had not left her side since the attack. He was pale. "What does it feel like to get shot?"

"I don't recommend it," said Nellie in a controlled voice. "Chocolate is definitely better." She managed a wink.

"Swiss," Natalie added longingly. Her trips to Harrods always ended in the Imported Confectionery department.

"Could you feel the bullet going in?" Ted asked from a chair in the corner.

"It was more like being hit by a bus," Nellie replied. "The sensation was all over, not just one spot. The wound itself didn't start hurting until later."

"They're going to send a doctor to take the bullet out, right?" Reagan asked impatiently.

"One would assume so," put in Alistair, looking worried. "If our captors' intention was murder, we would all be dead already."

Nellie shifted her position on the mattress, wincing in pain. "Well, I hope they hurry up about it," she complained. "If I wanted to be tortured, I'd go to the opera."

Fiske spoke sharply to the four walls. "We need medical attention immediately. We have a gunshot wound that requires treatment."

"You're not going to get through to them by talking like an English professor," scoffed Reagan. *"Hey!"* she bawled. *"Get a doctor down here! She's in pain, thanks to you! What are you going to do about it?"*

There was a moment of silence as Reagan's echo reverberated around the cell. Then they heard the rattle and hum of the dumbwaiter system.

Everyone but Nellie and Ted rushed into the main room. Reagan threw open the small door, and they looked inside.

There sat a glass of water and two Tylenol tablets.

Alistair's cane hand shook with agitated disbelief. "They can't be serious!"

"I'm afraid they are," said Fiske in a low voice. "They're serious about wanting young Nellie to suffer."

"Ow!"

"Hold still," Sinead ordered. "And don't be such a baby." She dabbed at the angry red mark behind Ian's ear. "Cat scratches are prone to infection, you know."

"And that's *my* fault?" Ian raged. "Why don't you lock that animal in the cellar? Or, better still, send him to a violin string factory! *Ow!* What *is* this stuff—acid?"

"My own concoction," she replied cheerfully. "Amy and I use it on our blisters when we do marathon training. Soothing, right?"

"They practice this kind of soothing in the Lucian stronghold—during *interrogations*."

The phone rang in the comm. center. Ian consulted the monitor. "It's Dan." He pressed a button. "Kabra here."

Dan's voice crackled through the attic. "Don't say it like that," he complained. "Your name still gives me heartburn. I got your message. What's the big news?"

"Dan, it's me," Sinead spoke up. "Ian and I have been analyzing the footage of the attack on Nellie. We think we've found something."

"Can you put it through to my phone?" Dan requested.

"Already done. Watch." She began the video feed. "You can't see the guards' faces through their masks. But when I freeze it here—" The image isolated the man with the crossbow, zooming in on the back of his neck. Sinead brought it into focus, and, four thousand miles away, Dan watched the magnified picture sharpen—the tag on the inside collar of the jailer's jacket.

"A label?" he questioned.

"If it's a small regional outerwear manufacturer, we might be able to narrow down where the hostages are being held."

"I guess it's something to go on," said Dan, not sounding terribly convinced.

"Where's Amy?" Ian put in. "Will you please get her to call that Evan character? He rings here twenty times a day. He's either the most mule-headed person who ever lived, or he really likes your sister. She has to have mercy on him — on all of us!"

"Amy's pretty busy," Dan told him. "She's at the library, trying to figure out when the real 'Medusa' might have been stolen from the Uffizi and replaced with that copy."

"If anybody can do it, Amy can," said Sinead. "She's a whiz at research."

Dan was not so sure. "One of the guards told me the Uffizi has never been robbed in living memory — until we did it, I mean. If somebody boosted a painting, it sure isn't going to be in any library book."

"What are you three guys doing?" asked Sinead.

"Jonah's with the mayor of Florence, getting the key to the city. Hamilton's helping Amy. I'm" — the voice faltered—"I'm just picking up a few things we need."

Dan ended the call and pocketed his phone. *Picking up a few things,* he had told Sinead and Ian. *Like thirty-nine.*

Amy would blow a gasket if she found out. But just watching the video clip of the shooting was all the confirmation Dan needed that what he was doing was absolutely necessary. Sure, Nellie was alive. Sure, Vesper One had just been making a statement. *This* time. Sooner or later, the guy was going to feel the need for a stronger statement. And people were going to wind up dead.

Amy was wrong about one thing: Vesper One did not hold *all* the cards in this lethal game. He had the hostages, sure. Yet only Dan's photographic memory had the recipe for Gideon Cahill's master serum.

Dan knew the myriad reasons against it. It was too dangerous; no one should have that much power. The mere fact that such a formula existed, and was therefore up for grabs, might reignite the treachery and feuding of the Clue hunt.

Those arguments made sense—or at least they had yesterday. Nellie's shooting changed everything. Now the stakes were even higher. Sky high.

Another difference: He was finding it hard to care anymore.

If enough bad stuff happens, the bad becomes normal. Risks aren't risks when the consequences are no worse than your regular life.

Dan had been only four when his parents died. He'd been so young that now he couldn't even be certain if he remembered the actual pain of their loss or the pain he'd felt hearing about it as he grew older. But for about thirty terrible seconds yesterday, Amy and Dan had believed Nellie was dead. There was no confusion over how *that* had felt — a toxic cocktail of grief and rage.

He had watched the video of the attack over and over again — even after he'd learned that the shooting had not been fatal. Amy said he'd become obsessed with it, that it was clouding his mind. But for Dan, the footage made everything crystal clear.

He would re-create Gideon's serum, and he would use the power it gave him to destroy the Vespers' plan and free the hostages.

That's what he was doing south of the Arno, in an old district dotted with odd shops and studios. He had already found iron solute and a solution containing ions of tungsten from a tiny machine shop, and myrrh from a Chinese herbalist. He knew it was going to take time to collect some of the rare ingredients, like the raw liquid silk of a *Bombyx mori* caterpillar, native only to Asia. But if Gideon Cahill could make it happen five hundred years ago, then Dan Cahill could get the job done in the twenty-first century, with the aid of a cell phone and Internet access.

Next on the list — amber.

A jewelry shop . . .

CHAPTER 13

Cahills—did you enjoy our little movie? I trust you didn't overdo it on the popcorn.

If we do not receive the real "Medusa" in 96 hours, you will be watching the sequel. This one will not have such a happy ending.

Vesper One

Amy sat at the ancient wooden table in the research section of the Biblioteca Nazionale Centrale di Firenze, the largest library in Italy. Piles of books surrounded her, and an assortment of printed photocopied documents lay scattered among them—police files on art thieves, and known buyers and sellers of stolen paintings.

Somewhere in all this reading material was the answer that could lead her to the real "Medusa."

Thousands of pages to be examined, more than half not even in English, and all she could do was stare at the tiny screen of the Vesper phone.

Ninety-six hours—four days. It wasn't much time when lives hung in the balance, and Vesper One had already proved that his terrible threats were one hundred percent legitimate.

She choked up for an instant, thinking of Nellie's face, twisted in agony.

What if we can't do it?

McIntyre had acted as if Amy and Dan taking the lead in this crisis was the most natural thing in the world. Yet learning kung fu and turning the attic into a comm. center didn't magically transform you into a leader. She was barely managing to keep her relationship with Evan from falling apart. How could she be expected to carry the weight of seven lives on her shoulders? *If* seven lives were all that was at stake! Amy had a sinking feeling that kidnapping was just a tool to the Vespers. They had bigger plans, awful plans.

But plans for what?

It was terrifying not to know what she was up against—like a chess game where the board or any one of the pieces might turn out to be a bomb.

Where was Dan? He was supposed to meet her here. She could certainly use another pair of eyes to help her go through all this material. Right now it was just Amy and Hamilton. Hamilton was loyal, and a tireless worker. But around a library, he was about as useful as silk gloves to a snake.

He teetered into the room, a tower of large ancient tomes in his arms. "Here's the stuff you asked for from the rare books department." He set the load heavily down on a free space on the table, kicking up a huge dust cloud.

Amy watched, amused, as the whitish puff swirled around him like a halo. "You look like a dust angel."

Hamilton laughed on a sneeze. "Yeah, kind of like those Mud Angel guys—" He noted the blank expression on her face. "You know—from that book on the Uffizi. They had this huge flood, and all these paintings got soaked. So the Mud Angels fixed them up."

Amy pounced on the thick volume Hamilton was pointing to and speed-read her way through the 1966 flood. Hamilton was right! With millions of artworks and rare books in danger from the worst flooding since the sixteenth century, the *Angeli del Fango*—Mud Angels—moved the entire collection to dry havens in a series of churches and public buildings around Florence. Thanks to their heroic efforts, many of the affected works were saved.

"Hamilton, you're a genius!" Amy exclaimed.

Hamilton looked vaguely pleased. "Told you."

"The 1966 flood was the only time the 'Medusa' was out of the gallery," Amy reasoned. "Even if it never got wet, it still would have been removed with all the rest! Then, while it was sitting in a church, someone swapped it with a forgery!"

Hamilton nodded, impressed. "How do we find where it is now? That was almost fifty years ago."

"At least we've got a place to start—the Mud Angels."

"Yeah, but all we know is what they did," Hamilton reasoned. "We don't know their names and addresses or anything like that."

Amy smiled. "These guys put together the biggest mass rescue in the history of art. I'll bet the Janus know exactly who they are." She took out her phone. "Let's call Jonah."

The key to the city of Florence was about two feet long, and painted a garish gold.

Hamilton was fascinated by it. "Wow! How big is the lock?"

Jonah laughed. "There *is* no lock, cuz. It's an honorary gig. Back in my crib in LA, I've got a whole shed full of keys from different cities. Want to know the kicker? I can't get at them. The gardener lost the key to the shed."

They were in Jonah's limo, en route to Peretola Airport, where Jonah's plane was parked. The star's Janus connections had come through once again. The secure fax machine aboard the G6 had already received a hundred and twenty-seven pages of highly classified information—the complete Janus file on the Mud Angels.

Jonah tapped on the glass partition that separated the chauffeur from the passenger area. "Just take us right out onto the tarmac," he instructed. "We called ahead, so the airport cops are down with it."

The car was admitted through a security gate into the private airfield. They tooled around the small terminal building, where an appalling sight met their eyes.

Jonah's jet was surrounded by a mass of humanity, hundreds strong, swarming the craft from nose to tail.

"Back up!" Jonah ordered sharply.

The driver threw the limo into reverse, and they retreated into the cover of the building.

Hamilton was bug-eyed. "Who *are* those people?"

Jonah held his head. "Man, I should have known it was a mistake to say I'd be leaving town soon! Why do fans have to be so literal?"

"Are they going to let us go get the faxes?" Hamilton asked.

Jonah stared at him. "You're kidding, right?"

"What do we do?"

"First," Jonah said thoughtfully, "we get a do-rag on that blond hair of yours. . . ."

When the limo drove out onto the tarmac toward Jonah's plane, the crowd reaction was a stampede.

"Jonah! *Ti amo!*"

"Stay in Firenze!"

"Gangsta *mio*!"

"Jonah!"

There was no response from the limo. All the fans saw of their idol was a tiny sliver of red bandanna through a two-inch gap of open window.

As the surging throng drew closer, the driver stepped on the gas. The big car pulled away from the jet, circled it, and headed back around the terminal building. The mass oozed after it like a giant amoeba.

On the other side of the concourse, a lone figure stepped out of the janitors' exit and looked around furtively. He wore track pants and a matching warm-up jacket, both at least three sizes too large.

Jonah watched as the limo drew the crowd away and then made a run out to his plane. Just before he ducked inside, he caught a glimpse of the car, stalled now, completely besieged by screaming fans. He could just make out the sight of Hamilton, squeezed into Jonah's jeans, being drawn out through the window feetfirst.

Oh, well, Hamilton was Tomas, and they were known to be strong and resilient. And, Jonah hoped, fast runners.

CHAPTER 14

127 pages of Janus documents on the Mud Angels.

 68 pages of police records on art thieves and known buyers and sellers of stolen art.

  1 large table.

  4 Cahill cousins.

"Okay," said Amy, "we read these files, and nobody gets up from this table—not even to go to the bathroom—until we've figured out who took the 'Medusa,' who has it now, and where we have to go to get it back."

"I can't read," Hamilton complained. "My eyes are swollen shut."

"Sometimes you have to take one for the team, yo," Jonah told him.

"I didn't take one for the team," said Hamilton through clenched teeth. "I took one for *you*. And if it gets back to my old man that a Holt was kicked around by a bunch of ten-year-old girls, I'll have to find another family!"

"Cut it out," Dan snapped, his face pinched. "Bad

stuff happens to all of us because of the family we were born into." The serum was very much on his mind — seven ingredients collected, thirty-two to go. "Let's just do this. Think of your sister, Hamilton. Or Phoenix. Or Nellie."

The four dove into the dossiers, and silence fell in the hotel suite. Their world became a blizzard of data — names, addresses, dates of birth, career highlights, prison records. Every random fact and mundane footnote had to be given full concentration. There was no way of knowing which casual detail would turn out to be the one that would lead them to the "Medusa." Would it come soon, or take hours — even days? Would it come at all?

After the first hour, all four had splitting headaches. By the third, Amy's ban on bathroom breaks had to be lifted.

Dan was returning from one of these when he caught a glimpse of a profile Jonah had just tossed onto the growing discard pile.

"Hey, that guy's in here twice."

It got Amy's attention. "There's another file with his name?"

Dan shook his head. "Not the name; the face."

"The pictures are faxed," Hamilton noted. "You can't see much."

"If Dan recognizes that guy, then it's the real thing." Amy picked up the discards. "Let's find him."

About halfway through the stack, the second file

emerged. Despite the blotchy fax quality, all four searchers had to admit that the faces matched.

The first was an entry on a watch list from the Arma dei Carabinieri — the Italian national police force. It contained information on one Alberto Sudem, who was suspected of being a buyer of stolen works of art. According to the notes, Sudem had dropped out of sight in the 1980s and was presumed dead. The other was one of the Janus secret files on the Mud Angels — Gregor Tobin, born 1937, a fabulously wealthy art collector currently living in a large palazzo on the shores of Lake Como.

Amy's eyes were alight with excitement. "It has to be him! He was a Mud Angel, so he had access to the 'Medusa.' And the Italian police have him on an art theft watch list."

"It also says they think he's dead," Hamilton pointed out.

"Who are you going to believe, yo?" Jonah challenged. "The Janus or a bunch of cops? It's the same face, the same guy. It's Gregor Tobin! Alberto Sudem must be an alias or something."

"Wait a minute," said Dan. He flipped over a file and began to scribble on the back.

ALBERTO SUDEM
A. SUDEM

He looked at the other three. "That's 'Medusa' spelled backwards."

Amy nodded slowly. "He created his alias based on his favorite stolen piece—or maybe his first. Where's Lake Como?"

"Up by Milan," Jonah supplied. "Did an outdoor concert there once, back in the day. The views are off the chain—mountains, water, real tourist brochure stuff."

Dan spoke up. "Aren't you forgetting something? We can't just knock on this guy's door and accuse him of boosting the 'Medusa.' Even if he admits it, he's not going to hand it over."

Amy set her jaw. "If we stole from one of the most secure museums in Europe, we can steal from Gregor Tobin. We just need a way inside."

"Not another window-washing job!" groaned Hamilton.

"This time," Amy promised, "we're going to be invited."

CHAPTER 15

"Three thousand years old and still looking good."

Dan hunched over the laptop in the Cahills' Lake Como hotel suite, watching the images download from the comm. center in Attleboro. One by one, hi-res pictures of the gold Sakhet statue appeared on the screen. He and Amy had acquired the ancient sculpture two years before, when the Clue hunt had taken them on a wild ride through Egypt.

Amy was on the phone with Ian, who was acting as official photographer. "Take it from all angles," she advised him. "We want to give Tobin a three-hundred-and-sixty-degree view."

"Check," came Ian's voice from four thousand miles away. "What if he's not interested?"

"He'll be interested. The Janus file says he's gaga over Egyptian art."

Ian sighed wanly. "I once had the means to be gaga over art—before I found myself in a country where the standard of beauty is toaster waffles shaped like cartoon characters."

Dan flashed Amy a sign. All twelve photographs had been received.

"Thanks, Ian. We'll be in touch." She broke the connection and joined her brother at the computer. "Here's Tobin's e-mail address."

Dan opened a blank message and attached the photographs. "What are we going to tell the guy? We found this ancient Egyptian sculpture in the garbage? So we threw a dart at a map and flew halfway around the world on the off chance there'd be somebody there who would want to buy it?"

"Let me." Amy began to type on the keypad:

Mr. Tobin,

My young brother and I have acquired the ancient Egyptian statue that you see in these pictures. We believe it is an exceptionally well-preserved example of New Kingdom sculpture dated approximately to 1400 B.C. We would be most grateful for your expert opinion. We will be in Lake Como for one more day.

Amy Cahill

She looked up at Dan. "What do you think?"

"It's stupid," was his judgment. "What do we want with his expert opinion? We already know it's a Sakhet."

Amy shook her head in exasperation. "The statue isn't important. What we need is a ticket into the house so we can find the 'Medusa.'" She hit SEND. "Now all we have to do is wait for an invitation."

They left the hotel and took a stroll along the paved promenade at the lakeshore. Even Dan, who never noticed scenery, had to admit the place was stunning in its beauty — the water a flat blue calm surrounded by soaring mountains, rocky cliffs, and the historic buildings of Como itself.

Amy pointed to a modern chrome-and-glass villa set atop a high bluff. "That's Tobin's place," she told her brother.

"Pretty sweet." Dan followed the line of the rock down to a boat mooring on the lake below the house. "That must be his private dock. I'll bet there's an elevator. Rich guys aren't into stairs."

"That'll be our way out once we've got the 'Medusa,'" Amy decided. "Jonah and Hamilton can rent a boat and pick us up there."

As they followed the rail along the lakeshore, they came upon a retaining wall with a small alcove. In it was the carved frieze of a seated figure in Roman garb. A bronze plaque read: GAIUS PLINIUS CAECILIUS SECUNDUS

Dan made a face. "Get a load of the guy with the funny name."

"I think that's Pliny the Younger, the famous Roman writer," Amy supplied. She bent down to read the English portion of the information tablet. "Right. In A.D. 79, Pliny chronicled the destruction of Pompeii by the eruption of Mount Vesuvius. It's one of the earliest eyewitness accounts of a major disaster."

Dan yawned. "Doesn't this remind you of the clue hunt? You know—you telling me a bunch of boring stuff, and me not listening?" When she didn't snap back at him, he turned to look at her. She was very still, her expression thoughtful and distant. "What?"

From the pocket of her jeans, Amy produced the tiny charred notebook that had been salvaged from the fire at Grace's house two years before. She took it out of the Ziploc and riffled carefully through the brittle pages to the entry that had caught their attention before:

VSP 79 PUNY DESCRIBED FIRST TEST

"Dan—that's not 'puny'! It only looks like a 'U' because the 'L' and the 'I' are smudged together! It's 'PLINY'! 79 was the year Vesuvius erupted, and 'VSP' means it has something to do with the Vespers!"

Dan whistled. "Burying an entire city in lava and hot ash—sounds like a pretty Vesper thing to do." He shook his head. "But no one can 'test' a volcano. They erupt when they erupt."

Amy nodded in agreement. "Besides, there were no Vespers in A.D. 79. They started when the Cahills did."

Her brother frowned. "Grace had to know that. Why would she jump to a conclusion that makes no sense?"

Amy tried to be logical. "The Vespers didn't commit seven kidnappings to get a free painting. They have big plans. But so far we've made zero progress figuring out what those plans might be."

"If you're trying to cheer me up," Dan informed her, "then telling me what a crummy job we're doing isn't the best way to make it happen."

"Don't you see?" Amy gestured toward the alcove monument. "*This* is the missing piece in what we know about the Vespers!"

"Some guy who wrote about a volcano?"

"The connection between an ancient disaster and a secret organization that wouldn't start for another millennium and a half." She held up the notebook. "That's what Grace understood, and we have to find out."

"There's another possibility," Dan suggested. "What if Grace was just plain wrong? She was pretty sick near the end. Maybe she wasn't thinking straight."

Amy wasn't convinced. During the Clue hunt, their grandmother had planted hints in their minds years before Amy and Dan had ever learned of their family's place in history. In a few instances, she'd laid the groundwork for them decades prior to their births.

When it came to Cahill business, Grace was *never* wrong.

CHAPTER 16

The letter had been slipped under the door of their hotel suite sometime during the night.

Miss Cahill,
I would be honored to host you and your brother at 2 P.M. at my villa. And I would be pleased to offer my opinion of your sculpture.
Until then,
Gregor Tobin

Dan was suspicious. "How did he find out where we were staying?"

Amy frowned. "I think that's the message inside the message. He wants us to know that he has a long reach—that he's rich and powerful."

"Like we'll see his giant mansion and assume he works at Burger King," scoffed Dan.

They spent the morning packing up their belongings so that everything could be loaded onto Jonah's plane in advance. The ideal getaway would be to grab the "Medusa" and take it directly from boat to car to jet, with no delays.

The man they were about to rob was not someone to be trifled with.

Gregor Tobin could have played Dracula in any Hollywood movie. The fangs would have to be added, but everything else was there — shiny black-dyed hair, gaunt features, sunken cheeks, pale skin.

"Welcome, new friends." The voice was deep and dead flat. "I've had my chef prepare a light luncheon. Please join me."

Amy and Dan murmured a polite acceptance and followed him into a sun-drenched breakfast room, where a small table was set for three.

Dan picked up a toast point topped with a mysterious spread. He took a cautious sniff — liver — and slipped it back onto the tray.

"May I ask what brought you to *my* door?" Tobin inquired, applying himself to a dainty sandwich. "There are many other art experts. This is Italy."

Amy looked shy. "We wanted to meet you. We heard you were one of the Mud Angels back in the sixties."

Tobin seemed pleased. "Why, yes. I didn't know anyone remembered that. A terrible time. So many masterpieces lost."

I'll bet, Amy thought cynically. *Some to water damage, and at least one stuck to your greasy fingers.*

"You guys were, like, heroes!" Dan exclaimed.

"Every citizen of Florence was heroic," Tobin said distractedly. His eyes never left Amy's over-size backpack, which leaned against her chair. "Please excuse my boldness. I must confess I'm anxious to see what you have brought me. It puzzles me that I have not heard of this object before. How did two such young people come into possession of it?"

"You're asking if it's stolen," Amy said. "Would that make it less attractive to you, or more?"

He looked at her sharply. "What an interesting young lady. But you still haven't answered my question. Where did you get it?"

"It's not stolen." Amy told him. "We inherited it from our grandmother, Grace Cahill."

"Grace Cahill!" Tobin's thick single brow leaped. "That name is well known in the art world!" His eyes narrowed. "As her heirs, you must know the quality and value of her collection. What is the real purpose of this visit?"

Amy launched into the explanation she and Dan had cooked up together. "According to the will, we can't touch one penny of the estate until we are both twenty-five."

Tobin smiled. "So the piece *is* stolen."

Dan bristled. "She just told you that it isn't."

"But it is. You have stolen it from your future selves. Tea?"

Amy held out her cup for a refill. "Mr. Tobin, our grandmother's lawyer keeps us penniless when we're worth millions. We don't want to sell off our inheritance. We have no choice."

"Very well. Show me the statue, and we shall see if we can do business."

Amy reached for the zipper of her bag.

"Maybe we shouldn't sell," Dan put in nervously. "If McIntyre sees it's missing, he could have us arrested."

Amy looked as if she were about to cry. "Could we take some time to think about it?"

"Of course. Perhaps you'd like to tour my gallery — see the fine company your piece will be keeping."

Amy re-shouldered her pack, and the Cahills followed Tobin up a broad cantilever staircase to the top floor of the villa, a vast room with a magnificent floor-to-ceiling window overlooking Lake Como.

"Cool house," approved Dan.

"Thank you." Tobin smiled. "Traditional architecture has its grandeur, but there is nothing like a modern design that admits light. It makes art come alive."

Tobin's collection may not have been as large as the Uffizi's, but it was every bit as impressive. There were works from all time periods and from every corner of the world. There were prehistoric drawings cut from caves, and Jackson Pollock canvases that covered entire walls. There were medieval tapestries, Grecian urns, Roman busts on pedestals, African and Eskimo indigenous art, and Mesopotamian cuneiforms. There were even famous historical artifacts — a genuine Roman chariot, all gilt carving and completely intact, and a coat of arms that had hung in the court of King Richard the Lionheart.

What was not there was Caravaggio's "Medusa."

When the collector went over to speak to a burly security man stationed by a Giotto altarpiece, Dan sidled up to his sister. "Where's old double-ugly?"

"There must be a secret room," Amy whispered back, "a covert gallery for the stolen stuff. Keep an eye out for hidden doors or panels, anything suspicious."

Dan did a quick 360. "You mean like one room with two thermostats?"

Amy tried not to stare. Her brother was right. There was a unit by the door. That would set the temperature in the gallery. So what was the purpose of the other one, the one on the east wall? It had to control the climate *somewhere else.*

And then she knew. Right beside the second thermostat hung a large Renoir, a luminous café scene on a canvas at least six feet high and three feet wide. The frame was ornate and massive.

Almost imperceptibly, she inclined her head in the direction of the huge work. "Dan — what does this remind you of? Not the picture — the size and shape?"

Dan nodded slowly. "A door. The secret gallery is behind the painting."

The conversation ended abruptly with the return

of Gregor Tobin. "And what has you two so absorbed and excited?"

"We've made our decision," Amy told him. "We're going to sell you the statue." She shrugged out of her backpack and reached inside.

The collector's anticipation turned to bewilderment when she came up with what looked like a lollipop. "Is this a joke?"

Amy broke the stick detonator off Sinead's smoke bomb and threw both pieces to the floor. The fog was dense and instantaneous.

Tobin cried out in shock. Amy grabbed Dan's shoulders and dragged the two of them down to the cool marble. The Cahills pulled the breathing filters from their pockets and covered their noses. Tobin took one whiff of the knockout gas and collapsed beside them. A thump from across the room indicated that the security guard was also unconscious.

"Stay low!" Amy hissed. "I don't know how much we can trust these masks!"

The two crawled to the large Renoir painting and began to haul on the heavy frame. It wouldn't budge. Amy felt a stab of fear. What if they were wrong?

Dan produced a pocketknife and held it to the canvas.

Amy grabbed it out of his hand. "Don't you dare! It's a *Renoir*!"

"Let Tobin restore it if he's such a big-shot Mud Angel!"

Desperately, Amy reached behind the picture to get a better grip on the frame. Her finger brushed against a small hard lump. A button? She pressed it. There was an electronic click, and the Renoir swung away from the wall. Inside, dimly lit, was a second art gallery.

It was smaller than the main collection, but the pieces seemed to be of equal quality. She had a fleeting wish that Jonah was with them — a Janus would have a better sense of what they were looking at.

Then something familiar caught her eye. It was a picture of three people seated around a grand piano.

"Dan — that's 'The Concert' by Vermeer! It was taken in a robbery from the Gardner Museum in Boston in 1990! It's considered the most valuable stolen painting in the world!"

"Amy, stop sightseeing!" he snapped. "There's only one stolen painting I care about!"

They searched the room, passing mummies smuggled out of Egypt, Grecian marbles illegally removed from the pediment of the Parthenon, and stolen paintings by Gainsborough, Van Eyck, and Monet.

Dan spotted it first, Caravaggio's "Medusa" recessed in an alcove with a lone spotlight on the horror-stricken features.

"There it is. I don't know why I expected this one to be better-looking."

The two wasted precious seconds taking in the hideous details of Caravaggio's masterpiece. After creating three Janus fakes in order to get their hands on the Uffizi piece that itself turned out to be a fake, surely this had to be the real thing—the one that would satisfy Vesper One enough to release the hostages.

Dan snatched the shield off the wall, and the two managed to cram it into Amy's large knapsack. The rounded edges pressed the vinyl material to the limit.

"Looks like we boosted a manhole cover," he commented as she shrugged into the straps.

In the main gallery, somebody groaned.

"Let's get out of here!" Dan exclaimed. "Where's that elevator to the boat dock?"

"Definitely not up here," Amy replied. "It must be downstairs."

Holding the filters to their faces, they slipped through the Renoir door to the main gallery. The smoke was dissipating. The guard was still out, but Tobin was beginning to stir.

The collector blinked away his dizziness enough to take in the sight of Amy and Dan emerging from the secret gallery.

"Thieves!" he accused.

"Call the cops!" Dan tossed over his shoulder as they headed for the stairs. "They'll have a field day in this place!"

Amy set her foot down on the top cantilever step and froze. Vibrations were coming from below. Running feet. More than one set. Looking down, she caught a glimpse of two more security guards rushing to investigate their employer's cry.

Amy grabbed Dan's hand, whipped the two of them around, and headed back toward the main gallery. "Change of plan! We have to find another way out!"

"There *is* no other way out!" Dan croaked.

They ran the full length of the gallery, hoping against hope that an alternate staircase would magically appear. At last, they were in front of the picture window. Both looked down. At the base of the cliff, far below, a speedboat bobbed in the gleaming blue water—Jonah and Hamilton in the getaway craft. Between the two pairs of Cahills lay eighty vertical feet of steep, craggy terrain.

There was only one way to bring the four together.

"How's your rock climbing?" Amy asked in a shaky voice.

In answer, Dan began to kick at the glass. The window rattled but didn't break.

The two security men reached the top of the stairs.

"Stop them!" Tobin roared.

The Cahills made a double run in an attempt to breach the window. They bounced off painfully.

"We need something heavier!" Dan gasped.

Hearts sinking, they surveyed their surroundings. The gallery was filled with art, not bricks! What could they use to get themselves through the window?

At the same instant, two sets of eyes fell on the Roman chariot.

CHAPTER 17

Neither said a word. There wasn't time. The decision flashed between them as if by radar. Amy and Dan got behind the gilt chariot and braced themselves to push.

Would two-thousand-year-old wheels even move? They were going to find out.

Tobin had stopped yelling and was running toward them now, the two security men right behind him.

Amy and Dan heaved with all their might. With a groan, the ancient wheels began to turn.

"Faster, Dan!" Amy wheezed. They could feel pounding footsteps approaching on the marble floor.

The chariot was heavy and gained speed agonizingly slowly. But once it began to freewheel, there was no stopping it.

Crash!

The picture window disintegrated into a million shards of glittering glass that fell like a sun shower. The chariot rumbled out onto the slope, toppled on its side, and got hung up against an outcropping of rock. Another few inches, and it would have plunged over the edge and taken out Jonah, Hamilton, and their boat.

Amy and Dan jumped past the windowsill and began to work their way down the rough terrain of the cliff, using rocks and bushes as handholds, relying on anything that looked like it might support their weight.

They had not descended very far when Amy saw a leg swing over the lip of the bluff. A security guard. The second man followed quickly.

She peered over her shoulder and immediately regretted it. Lake Como was still sixty feet below. A slip from here, and she would be a grease spot on the deck of their getaway boat, annihilating the "Medusa" in her backpack and destroying seven more lives besides her own.

Dan was faster than her, scrambling down like a monkey. She felt a twinge of resentment along with her terror. The dweeb's advantage was that he was too mindless to think about what would happen if he fell.

"Hurry up, Amy! I thought Sinead was teaching you to climb!"

"I said she was teaching me!" Amy shot back. "I never said I learned!"

With alarming suddenness, the scrub pine trunk under her right foot gave way, and she was sliding, picking up speed, clawing at the rocks and weeds as they moved past. She heard her own scream as if it were coming from someone else.

When the exposed root trapped her ankle, at first she thought gravity would flip her over and dangle her upside down. She put every ounce of strength into her fingertips and dug them into exposed earth on the cliff.

She lurched to a halt alive but still a good twenty-five feet above the getaway craft. She looked down again and saw Dan being helped aboard by Jonah and Hamilton. And then, a more alarming sight—Gregor Tobin appeared on his dock and climbed over the gunwale of a gleaming powerboat.

The lead guard was just a few feet above her now. His flailing boot passed within inches of her wind-blown hair.

Dan's voice reached her. "Amy—jump!"

"I'm too high!"

"I'll catch you!" Hamilton shouted. "I promise!"

Amy was never quite sure why she believed him so completely. Maybe it was a Cahill thing. That wasn't goofy, irresponsible Hamilton Holt down there: It was the full might and muscle of the Tomas branch.

She heard a grunt from her pursuer—very close. In another second, he'd be upon her.

She let go. The free fall was like a carnival ride. It lasted longer than she expected, long enough for her to wonder if she'd missed the target. She opened her eyes and saw the rocks hurtling to meet her.

Panic-stricken, she braced for impact.

And then Hamilton caught her, just as he had said

he would. Her weight knocked him over. The two of them wound up flat on their backs on the deck.

Her stammered gratitude was drowned out by the roar of the outboard engine as they plowed away from the shore, prow rising, kicking up a spray.

"Hang on, homeys!" Jonah bellowed from behind the wheel.

A sleek white shape fell in behind them, keeping pace. It was Tobin's speedboat, the collector himself at the controls.

They watched as he hefted a long, dark object and rested it on the windscreen, pointed in their direction.

"He's got a rifle!" Dan gasped.

Crack!

The bullet whined past Jonah's elbow, shattering his Perrier, which drained onto the console. "Man, the Wiz will *not* get whacked by some clown who couldn't even score a screen test!"

"Behind me, everyone!" Amy unzipped her backpack and pulled out the "Medusa." She held it up in front of all of them. "He won't risk shooting the painting!"

The rifle disappeared, but Tobin did not break off his pursuit.

"How are we going to get away from that guy?" Hamilton cried. "We'll never be able to dock with him on our tail!"

Dan moved forward and replaced Jonah at the helm. "I've got a plan!"

"That's my man!" The famous grin disappeared as Jonah took in the grim determination in Dan's features. The expression was as flat and emotionless as a naked skull.

Dan steered the hurtling boat directly toward the rocky shore. "Amy, hang on to the painting!"

"That's not a plan!" Jonah shouted. "That's suicide!" He tried to retake the wheel, but his cousin shoved him roughly away.

The throttle at maximum, Dan pointed the bow at a flat area between two large boulders. The speedboat threaded the needle and rocketed out of the water up a grassy embankment. Briefly, they were aloft, crushing small saplings as they came down. The fiberglass hull cracked open like an egg, sending them flying. The contents of Amy's open pack scattered in all directions. Passports landed in the mud. Hamilton caught the Vesper phone in midair just as it was about to hit a tree.

Amy landed flat on her back in a bed of moss, holding the "Medusa" high and away from harm.

* — * — * — * — *

On the water, Tobin veered sharply off, scarcely able to believe his eyes. Those four young people were surely dead. And the Caravaggio would be in similar condition. No one and nothing could survive such a crash.

It was a terrible loss for the art world.

CHAPTER 18

Hamilton dabbed a tissue at the cut under his eye. "Except for the time I met the Great Khali, that was the coolest thing I've ever done!"

The foursome, only slightly the worse for wear, stood on the tarmac of the small airfield outside Milan, transferring their luggage from the limo to Jonah's jet for the flight back to Florence.

"You didn't do anything, yo," Jonah seethed. "It was done to all of us by the freak show with the nerve to complain that the family branches are too violent!"

"We made it, didn't we?" Dan said quietly.

Amy patted her battered backpack, where the "Medusa" was concealed once more. "The important thing is we got what we came for. That's all that matters."

She peered past Hamilton's bulk at her brother. Dan was staring straight ahead, his eyes almost snakelike, focused on infinity. He had uttered barely a word during the hour-long limo ride.

He's receded into himself again, scuba diving in the depths of his own mind.

His heroics on Lake Como had secured their escape but could just as easily have gotten them all killed. Would the old Dan have dared to try something so reckless and self destructive?

Amy doubted it. His newfound dark side was in charge again.

She kept seeing his face as he'd steered for the ramp rock. His expression was not one of calculating risk. It was the breakneck abandon of someone who felt he had nothing to lose.

The chime of the Vesper phone jolted her back to reality. She took it out and examined the latest text from their enemy.

```
72 hours. Tick . . . tick . . . tick . . .

Don't give me the pleasure of punishing
another Cahill. I've been trying to cut
down.

Vesper One
```

Hamilton read over her shoulder. "Man, that guy's creepy."

Amy shook her head. "He'd need years of charm school to work his way up to creepy."

The phone emitted a chirp, and a new message appeared on the screen.

```
BATTERY LOW
20% of power remaining
```

"You guys have a charger, right?" Jonah asked.

Amy felt a stirring of unease. The smartphone had come with a power cable. She'd brought it to Italy. She'd been careful to pack it when they'd departed Florence. And this morning, when they'd left their Lake Como hotel, it had been safe in her knapsack.

Yet a search of the bag revealed no charger.

"Where is it?" Dan demanded.

The scene replayed itself in her head: the wreckage of the rented boat, the four Cahills replacing the strewn contents of her backpack. She remembered the wallet, the notebook, the cell phone, the airline tickets, the passports, the flashlight key chain.

She did not remember the charger.

"We must have lost it when the boat crashed."

Hamilton frowned. "If Vesper One sends instructions for the drop-off, but we never get them because the phone's dead . . ."

"We need that cable!" Dan exclaimed urgently.

"Chill, cuz," Jonah soothed. "They've got cell phone stores in Italy, too. We'll buy a new charger. My treat."

That was when fear began rising—when store after store after store along Milan's Via Vitruvio informed them that they had no power cable that would match the Vesper phone's unusual connection interface.

Hamilton called in. He'd taken the limo back to Lake Como to search the remains of the speedboat. There was no sign of the missing charger.

"It's probably at the bottom of the lake," he reported mournfully.

"When that phone runs out of power, we won't be able to follow Vesper One's orders anymore!" Dan raved. "If he thinks we're ignoring him, the next time he shoots one of our people, it'll be right between the eyes!"

"We're not done yet," Amy said determinedly.

"You're out of your mind, yo!" Jonah was beside himself. "We can't find the original, and we can't buy a new one. What's left?"

"We can invent our own," she told him.

Dan was pop-eyed. "Invent our own?"

"Well, not *us*," Amy amended. "But Sinead is an Ekat. Maybe she can whip something up."

"I'll never understand the American obsession with driving oneself," Ian observed. "As if it makes you a better person to risk life and property behind the wheel of a two-ton mechanical monster."

"This isn't London," chuckled McIntyre in the driver's seat of his Lincoln. "If you'd called a taxi, you'd still be waiting. And the problem we are attempting to solve is quite urgent. Have you got the list of equipment Sinead requires?"

"Right here in my hand," Ian said irritably. He did not relish the idea of being an errand boy for an Ekaterina. There was a time when the Kabras had servants to handle such mundane matters as this. But, of course, he was poor now.

He felt a twinge of guilt for complaining when his little sister was in a much worse predicament. His heart turned over in his chest.

The lawyer dropped him off at Attleboro Circuits, a sewer of a place with fly-specked windows. The last electronics shop Ian had patronized displayed a crest over the door proclaiming it to be SUPPLIER OF SMALL ELECTRONICS BY APPOINTMENT TO HIS ROYAL HIGHNESS THE PRINCE OF WALES.

This one bore a tattered cardboard sign that read NO SHIRT, NO SHOES, NO SERVICE.

It was no place for a Kabra, not even a poor one living in exile with a psychopathic cat.

He approached the counter and rang the bell with authority. The clerk turned around.

Evan Tolliver.

"You're Amy's cousin!"

"Yes, I am," Ian confirmed. "I have here a list of items—"

"Have you heard from her?" Evan interrupted. "Is she okay?"

"Her health is excellent."

"No, I mean—"

Ian sighed. "Why should you care? She promises to phone you, and she doesn't. You were nearly arrested, thanks to her. There's a message in there somewhere, don't you agree?"

Evan nodded sadly. "I kind of think so, too. But we were awesome together. She's smart, fun to be with, and not immature like most of the girls in our school. It's as if she has an automatic switch for when it's time to be serious—she can almost be old beyond her years at times. Where do you learn something like that?"

"I have no earthly idea," Ian lied. He slid the list across the counter. "Now then . . ."

Evan made no move to take it. His eyes were on the other paper, the one still in Ian's hand. It was a photograph of the Vesper phone and its unique interface.

"Hey, where'd you get a picture of a DeOssie smartphone?"

Ian frowned. "A what?"

Evan indicated the picture that Amy had sent from Lake Como. "DeOssie. They make ultra-secure phones, mostly for groups like the CIA and other government agencies. Regular people can't buy them." His eyes narrowed. "Does this have anything to do with Amy?"

Ian's mind raced. No ordinary person could acquire

a DeOssie phone. Yet Vesper One had managed it. How? The answer to that question might very well lead them to Vesper One himself. And once they had Vesper One, they could force him to release Natalie and the others.

Evan was the key. He'd recognized the DeOssie phone when even Sinead, an Ekaterina, hadn't. His knowledge of technology and computers could prove very useful.

"Take the rest of the day off," Ian invited. "I have a story to tell you. A long one."

Evan shook his head. "My shift just started."

"Get someone to cover," said Ian. "Amy needs you."

CHAPTER 19

A private jet wasn't the worst place to kill a few hours, but the four Cahill cousins barely noticed their sumptuous surroundings. As they waited for the thunderstorms that had closed Peretola Airport to move off, Amy barely tore her eyes from the power indicator on the Vesper phone. It was as if she believed she could prevent the bars from dwindling by the sheer force of her mind. Jonah buried himself in a pile of scripts he was reading to choose his next movie project, yet he spent most of his time on his iPad, staring forlornly at a picture of his cousin Phoenix. Hamilton pumped and curled a set of dumbbells with such wild abandon that he dented the bulkhead of the plane in three places.

Dan passed the time examining the latest—and, they hoped, genuine—"Medusa." It seemed identical to the forgery from the Uffizi—the same ugly, horrified face, snake hair, and spurting blood. You could almost hear the scream.

"If this is the real McCoy," he wondered, "then how

did Vesper One know the other one was a fake? They're exactly the same."

"Maybe he's an art connoisseur," Amy replied. "Just because you think video games are the highest form of human expression—"

She was teasing, trying to get a rise out of him, but the old Dan was increasingly hard to reach these days.

"You know I remember stuff." He cut her off in a wounded tone. "The Janus copies were a little different because they were made so fast. But this is a perfect match for the one we handed over. I'd bet all my collections on it."

"There are other ways to tell if a work is genuine," she mused. "X-rays and lab tests to determine the age and chemical makeup of the paint—that kind of thing."

"Yeah, but tests take time," Dan persisted. "The Vespers knew right away. I mean, we made the drop-off, and before we got halfway through lunch—" His voice cracked as he thought of the video—the way Nellie's body flinched as the bullet slammed into her. *More ingredients to find, a formula to recreate. The real "Medusa" doesn't change that. . . .*

"There must be something that tipped the Vespers off." When the answer came to Amy, it seemed so obvious that she couldn't believe it hadn't occurred to her before.

She flipped the shield over in Dan's lap, and the two of them examined the backing. It was black, and where the arm strap would have been was a rectangular expanse of raw wood, jagged at both ends. The studs that had once held the strip in place were all there, attesting to the sixteenth-century workmanship.

At first, they saw nothing worthy of note. But as their eyes focused on the wood and grew accustomed to its shading, it became apparent that some kind of message had been etched there. The characters were faint, many even worn away.

Amy reached for a pencil and a piece of scrap paper. Placing the page over the wood, she began to rub with the soft side of the lead, hoping to re-create what was written there. She and Dan watched, fascinated, as the letters began to appear.

"*This* is what the Vespers are looking for!" Amy exclaimed. Her triumph ebbed a little. "What does it mean?"

"Is it Italian?" asked Dan.

"Maybe," his sister replied. "It could be Latin, too. We can't be sure unless we have all of it."

Dan reached for his cell phone. "I'm going to text it to Atticus."

Amy stared at him. "Your online buddy? The little kid? What would he know about it?"

"You talk like he's still in diapers. At eleven, he's already forgotten more than you and I will ever know. He speaks, like, ten languages—including Italian *and* Latin. If anybody has a chance of understanding this, it's Atticus!"

"Okay," Amy conceded reluctantly. "But be careful what you say. If this kid is half as smart as you think, he might get a sense of what we're up against and call the cops because he thinks he's helping."

Dan laughed out loud. "That's the beauty of Atticus. When it comes to school stuff, he's a major prodigy genius dude. But at everything else, he's clueless." He texted the cryptic letters from the back of the shield and added the message:

need to borrow your great brain. this came in hw assignment. can you fill in blanks? think it might be italian or latin. should be right up your alley. everything is – dan

He hit SEND.

Amy was nervous. "I hope you know what you're doing. The last thing we need is to let outsiders in on what we're up to."

Her cell phone rang, and she checked the small screen. "It's Attleboro. Let's pray they've got good news about the charger." But when she answered the call, the voice on the other end of the line belonged to—

"Hi, Ames, it's me. Guess where I am right now!"

No. Impossible.

What was Evan doing in the comm. center?

"I know you're in my house, Evan," she replied carefully. "Uh—which part, exactly? I'm trying to get a mental picture."

"I'm in the attic. This comm. center is wild! You have your own *satellite?*"

No . . . no . . . no!

"Only a little one," Amy managed. "It's not really a comm. center. More like a den. For kicking back, watching TV—"

Ian's upper-class English accent replaced Evan on the line. "Amy, he knows."

"He knows what?" She was still hoping for damage control. Get Evan out fast, and never bring him upstairs again. Over time, maybe he could be convinced that what he saw was a kind of high-end home theater. . . .

"He knows everything," Ian supplied. "He's been fully briefed about the Cahills. It's all right—"

"All right for you, maybe!" Amy cut him off. "I left specific instructions to keep my personal life out of this. And what do you do? *The polar opposite of that!*"

"It's William McIntyre, Amy," announced an older, dignified voice. "Sinead is here as well. You're live in the comm. center."

"Wonderful," Amy said sarcastically. "What's the point of throwing a hissy fit without friends and family on hand to hear it?"

"We had every intention of respecting your wishes about Evan," the lawyer apologized. "But that was before he recognized the Vesper phone." He explained how DeOssie ultra-secure smartphone systems were only sold to the military and spy agencies. "Ian decided—and we all agree—that Evan's knowledge of this technology and this company could help us investigate the identity of Vesper One."

"It's our best lead so far," Sinead put in.

"What about the collar tag of the guy with the crossbow?" Amy asked.

"We're on that, too," Ian promised. "But this is bigger. If this mobile phone is so restricted that you need to be secretary of defense to buy it, how did Vesper One qualify? Is he a former military officer or ex-spy? At minimum, there's a Vesper on the DeOssie client roster somewhere. And for all we know, the whole company is controlled by the Vespers, and our people are being held somewhere in the DeOssie factory in upstate New York."

"Maybe you can get customer details or shipping addresses," Amy mused. "Tap some of our Cahill connections in government and the military."

"Your young man was correct when he told us of the smothering secrecy surrounding this entity," McIntyre said sadly. "Our contacts at the state department could not unearth a single DeOssie client. Ian's Lucian friends at CIA were likewise stymied. The Tomas have a three-star general, and even he lacks the necessary security clearance. It's possible that, given time, we could acquire the information—"

"Time is the one thing we *don't* have," Amy agreed grudgingly. "I'm going to Skype you from Dan's laptop, so we can all talk about this."

"You look good, Amy," Evan said in a quiet voice when the comm. center appeared on the screen.

"You, too." Amy was surprised by the surge of emotion. The video link only seemed to underscore the thousands of miles that separated her from a normal life. She had never felt farther from home.

But this was not the time to be distracted. Between Attleboro and the Gulfstream jet, a plan was cobbled together. Jonah and Hamilton would return to the United States to join Ian and Sinead on a nighttime expedition to check out the DeOssie factory. It was to be a spy mission, searching for client lists, shipping orders, service contracts—anything that might lead them to the identity of the Vespers and where they might be found. However, at the first sign that the hostages were there, it would convert to a rescue attempt.

"We should be with them, Amy," Dan urged. "This is more important than keeping Vesper One happy."

Amy looked at him. "Until we have our hostages safe and sound, *nothing* is more important than keeping Vesper One happy. We can't be an ocean away when the message comes in to hand over the 'Medusa.'"

"If the Vesper phone hasn't already died by then," added Hamilton. "What's the word on a new charger?"

Evan spoke up. "Sinead and I are on it. She's got the coolest electronics lab in the guest house—"

"There's nothing cool about what we're doing, Evan," Amy interrupted. "It's deadly serious—and I mean that literally. That wasn't a Nerf gun Nellie got shot with."

"Amy," McIntyre said gently. "Evan has been enormously helpful. He deserves our gratitude."

Amy relented. "I was trying to keep the Cahill stuff separate from us, Evan. Sorry you got mixed up in this mess."

"I *want* to be mixed up in this mess."

"You don't. Honestly."

"Ames, if this is part of who you are, then I need to be in on it," Evan said earnestly. "This whole side of you is really different. Not better, exactly, but—you know—impressive."

Amy sighed. *The clue hunt was impressive, too. Until the body bags started to pile up.*

She broke the connection only to have a new ringtone fill the Gulfstream's interior.

"Mine," Dan announced. The caller ID read: Rosenbloom, A.

He picked up the handset. "Atticus?"

"Dan—I got your e-mail!" Although Atticus was less than two years younger than Dan, there was a juvenile excitement in his voice that made him seem childish. "You won't believe this! Your homework—I'm standing less than a mile away from it!"

"What are you talking about?"

"The word puzzle," Atticus explained. "It is, in actuality, the Porta Sanavivaria."

"Which is . . ." Dan prompted.

"At the Colosseum—the *Roman* Colosseum? My brother's doing a semester in Rome. Dad's on sabbatical in India, so I went with Jake. We walk past the Colosseum every day!"

"So the Porto San—" Dan's tongue twisted.

There was hysterical laughter on the line. "A Portosan is a portable toilet. The Porta Sanavivaria was, in actuality, how you left the Colosseum if you were spared by the emperor. It's Latin for the Gate of Life."

"Roman Colosseum—Gate of Life," Dan repeated with a meaningful look at his sister. "Hey, if your brother's taking classes, what do you do all day?"

"I'm taking classes, too," the younger boy replied. "I didn't want to be bored in Italy, so I finished high school online in my spare time. But I also teach a seminar on dead languages. My students aren't very motivated," he finished in a disappointed tone.

"Kids these days," Dan commiserated. "Thanks for the info, Atticus. Let's get together when you're back in Boston." He hung up and turned to Amy. "So now we know—the name of a Roman Portosan is written on the back of the 'Medusa.' Why would the Vespers care about that?"

"I don't know," Amy admitted, "but we're going to

find out. Change of plan—" she called to Jonah. "Can you drop us off in Rome?"

"Yo, am I a movie star or a taxi service?" Jonah grumbled from the depths of the script pile.

"Technically, you're neither," Hamilton puffed, lifting weights again. "I mean, you're a *star* and you've made *movies* . . ."

Dan had a concern. "What if the text comes in to deliver the painting? We'll be in Rome, not Florence. And we won't have the plane after Jonah and Hamilton head back to the States."

"Vesper One gave us ninety-six hours," Amy reasoned. "Tomorrow's Thursday. So if we go to the Colosseum in the morning, we'll have plenty of time to get back to Florence at night to make the drop-off on Friday. It's usually less than three hours by train or car."

"Unless the guy changes his mind," Dan added nervously.

"He may be psycho," Amy replied evenly, "but he hasn't lied to us yet."

Dan nodded in grim agreement. Vesper One hadn't lied, all right. He'd promised consequences.

And look what he'd done to Nellie.

CHAPTER 20

The fever was back.

It had been moderate yesterday, but now Nellie was wracked with chills. She lay shivering on the cot, her face deathly white, her lips dry and cracked. She had pushed her jumpsuit off her shoulder, revealing an angry wound, raised, purple, and hot to the touch.

She was in bad shape, she was pretty sure, because she'd had no appetite since yesterday. When Nellie couldn't eat, something was seriously wrong. And even if she didn't understand it herself, she could see the urgency of the situation reflected in the faces of her fellow captives. Especially Phoenix, poor kiddo.

Fiske and Alistair consulted in whispers so the patient would not overhear.

"The situation is dire," Fiske admitted. "That wound is deeply infected, I fear. If the bullet is not removed soon, she could very well die."

Alistair was distracted with worry. "We could appeal to our jailers' humanity, but I honestly believe they don't have any." His cane hand twitched so badly that he rarely removed it from his jumpsuit pocket. "Is this sport to them, to inflict a minor wound and then to watch like spectators as it festers into something mortal?"

"We cannot allow it to happen," Fiske said firmly. "We must find a way to get through to our captors." His eyes fell on the remains of their most recent meal on the table. The plastic bottle of ketchup caught his attention. He smoothed out a paper napkin and wrote, squeezing out thin red lines:

SHE'S DYING

PLEASE HELP

He intercepted a look of wide-eyed horror from Phoenix and cursed himself for not being more careful with the message. The youngster had become quite attached to Nellie, and her condition terrified him.

It terrified all of them.

Fiske placed the napkin in the dumbwaiter and closed the door. A moment later, they heard the device creaking its way up out of the cell.

Nellie's feeble voice came from the bedroom. "Can somebody crank the heat in this meat locker?"

There were no more blankets, so Reagan yanked an armload of jumpsuits off the rack. She and Phoenix raced in and began to pile them on the patient.

Nearly twenty agonizing minutes had gone by before Fiske noticed the dumbwaiter rattling its way down again. He caught Alistair's attention and the two exchanged an anxious glance. In a few seconds they would have their answer, and it would literally be a matter of life and death.

They snatched the door open and stared in bewilderment. There on a stainless steel surgical tray sat a scalpel, tweezers, a bottle of alcohol, and a sterile bandage.

"Yes, but where's the doctor?" Alistair exclaimed impatiently.

Fiske took a deep breath. "There will be no doctor."

"Then what on earth could be the point of—" Light dawned on Alistair. "Absolutely not! If this is their idea of sick entertainment, I'll have no part of it."

Fiske regarded him gravely. If Nellie was to be saved, they would have to remove the bullet themselves.

It was a 50,000-seat stadium in the center of Rome. But *this* stadium—the Colosseum—was nearly two thousand years old, and most of it was still standing. It was the most impressive building of the Roman Empire, and one of the greatest tourist attractions in the world—as evidenced by the long line of visitors snaking through the velvet cordons stretching most of the way to the Arch of Constantine.

In the middle of this line stood Atticus Rosenbloom and his eighteen-year-old half brother, Jake.

Jake was not in a good mood. "I know you, Atticus. You don't care about seeing the Colosseum *again*.

You're just looking for an excuse to call Dan Cahill and tell him where you are."

Atticus was defensive. "You're turning your nose up at one of the world's true wonders?"

"No," Jake retorted, "I'm turning my nose up at standing in line for an hour to see something I've already seen every inch of. Seriously, Att, what is it with you and that Cahill kid? How much could someone like you have in common with someone like that? He's a mental midget compared to you."

"In actuality, Dan's very smart."

"Like his collection of photocopies of butt cheeks?" Jake challenged. "I hope you didn't send him yours."

Atticus grinned appreciatively. "There are different kinds of smart. It takes brains to be funny—not that you'd know anything about that. Dan's my friend. He's *cool*."

"Kids your age think anyone older is cool."

Atticus regarded him pointedly. "Not necessarily."

Jake snorted. "You're obsessed with the guy."

Atticus didn't argue. He *was* obsessed with Dan—but for a reason his brother knew nothing about. It certainly had nothing to do with being funny. In fact, it stemmed from a memory that was one hundred percent unfunny—the death of his mother.

Astrid Rosenbloom's last word—barely a whisper, spoken to Atticus alone through a demented haze—had been *Cahill*.

There had been more, but she'd been so weak,

bestowing her final, tortured breath upon those two syllables.

It couldn't be a coincidence. Dan was important somehow.

It had been Mom who'd directed Atticus to the gamers' chat room where he'd first encountered Dan. The two had become fast friends—never mind that Atticus was there as a chess player, and video gamer Dan didn't know castling from en passant. There was no question that Mom had sown the seeds of their friendship. But why? It was impossible to know. Soon after, she had become mysteriously ill and hadn't been making a lot of sense.

So Atticus had decided to be patient and hold on to the hope that her purpose would reveal itself in time. Besides, Dan was awesome. The eleven-year-old genius wasn't such a social butterfly that he could afford to throw friends away. In actuality, Dan was his only one.

Maybe Mom's grand plan had been nothing more than that: to ensure that her son didn't go through life as a brilliant hermit, isolated from the rest of humanity by his unique mind.

"We're almost at the entrance," Atticus told his brother. "I'm going to give Dan a call. He'll get a kick out of hearing where we are."

"Are you crazy?" Jake exclaimed. "It's five o'clock in the morning in Boston!"

"I have to catch him before he leaves for school." Atticus hit the number on his speed dial.

Next, something strange happened. There were quite a few rings. Then Dan answered, "Hello?" and the voice came from two places—from the phone, and from somewhere close by, farther back in the line. Bewildered, Atticus wheeled. There, about fifteen feet away as the queue wrapped around where the ropes were strung, stood none other than Dan himself, larger than life!

"Dan! Dan!" Atticus's high-pitched voice cut across the crowd. "Over here!" He ducked under the cord and rushed up to his friend. "Why didn't you tell me you were in Rome?"

"We just got here," Dan admitted, embarrassed, as the two exchanged a high five.

"Yeah, but why didn't you say you were coming?"

Dan shrugged. "It's kind of a family thing. This is my sister, Amy. Amy—Atticus."

"Come on, we have a place in line up ahead," Atticus invited. "You'll meet my brother, Jake."

——✲—*—*

With the clock ticking down to the time when the "Medusa" had to be handed over, Amy was grateful to be moved ahead in line—even if it meant sharing the day with Dan's oddball Internet buddy. Every minute was precious now.

The brothers Rosenbloom could not have been more different. Atticus was slight and dark, with owlish eyes behind large round glasses. The curly hair inherited from his African American mother was tightly woven into shoulder-length dreadlocks. Then there was Jake. Amy had a Colosseum to explore, a drop-off to make in another city, and seven hostages to worry about, not to mention a boyfriend back in the States. All that disappeared for a few seconds while she took a moment to appreciate the splendor that was Jake. He was at least six feet two, fairer, with sharp eyes and chiseled features.

"You're full of surprises today, Att," he accused, looking as if he smelled something ever so slightly unpleasant, something he could not quite put his finger on.

Amy noted his lack of enthusiasm. "We'll go off on our own as soon as we get inside. We don't want to intrude on your day."

"Are you kidding?" Atticus crowed. "We'll tour together! I know the Colosseum like the back of my hand. I'll be your guide!"

Dan shot Amy a look of unspoken communication. If Atticus could shorten their search . . .

Amy nodded. "Together, then."

If Jake didn't like it, he'd just have to get over himself.

"See how the ground level columns are Doric," Atticus lectured, pointing to the rounded face of the massive stone structure. "On the second level, the columns are Ionic, and on the third, Corinthian. Those are, in actuality, the three main styles of architecture employed during the Roman Empire."

Amy could see Dan's eyes glazing over. He wasn't much for museum tours — even coming from the friend he valued so much.

"The origins are Greek, of course," Atticus went on. "Most Roman architecture derives from Greek sources. . . ."

"When do we get to the part about people being eaten by lions?" Dan put in.

Jake cast a superior glance at Dan. "Those stories have been grossly exaggerated over the centuries. We now know that tales of Christians being thrown to wild carnivores are just myths."

"But the Colosseum was a place for blood sports." Atticus took up the narrative. "Gladiators fighting exotic animals and each other, beast pitted against beast. The floor of the arena was originally covered with sand to soak up the blood."

"Cool," said Dan, his interest reviving.

At the front of the line at last, they bought their tickets and entered the most famous stadium that had ever existed. Atticus led them through a long tunnel-like corridor, and they emerged into the arena.

"Whoa!" Dan breathed. "This is just like Foxboro, where the Patriots play! You know — if Foxboro was falling down."

Amy nodded in awe. The Colosseum was nearly two millennia old, a vast stone husk ruined by centuries of storms, earthquakes, and theft. But the size, the seating capacity, and the basic design were no different than a football stadium that could host a twenty-first-century Super Bowl. The fact that ancient people had created such a marvel was nothing short of astounding.

"In actuality," Atticus told Dan, "the Colosseum was superior to Foxboro in many ways. For example, it was covered. A huge canopy called a velarium provided protection from the sun."

"Whoa," Dan exclaimed. "This used to be the Roma-dome."

Atticus nodded. "And a capacity crowd could go in and out much faster than in a modern stadium. There are approximately eighty exits at ground level, accessed by the Colosseum's vomitoria."

Dan lifted three inches off the floor. *Vomitoria? What's that—the barfing section?"*

Atticus laughed so hard that he began to choke. For a super genius, Amy reflected, he had a sense of humor like—well, like *Dan's.*

Maybe that's why the two of them hit it off. . . .

Atticus wiped tears of mirth from his eyes. "A vomitorium has nothing to do with barfing. It's an exit tunnel built right into a tier of seating. The seats are mostly gone now, but you can still see where the vomitoria used to be."

"It's sort of about barfing," Dan argued. "You know, how the stadium vomits out the people."

Atticus turned his attention to the center of the arena. "The Colosseum floor is gone, so what we're looking at here are the passages and holding pens underneath. The Romans had a trapdoor in the middle of the ring so that new animals could be hoisted up and released right into the middle of the action. And over *here* . . ."

Dan followed his friend around the arena's perimeter, drinking in every gory detail of the Colosseum's violent history. Amy hung back with Jake, walking slowly. To her surprise, she'd seen more of the old Dan in the last half hour than in the entire two years since the Clue hunt. Atticus seemed to draw it out of him.

Jake definitely did not approve. As he watched the younger boys, his expression grew more sour — or perhaps the mysterious bad smell had become even worse.

"Now we know what our kid brothers have in common," she said, just to break the silence. "Dumb jokes and carnage."

"Att has a one-in-ten-million mind," Jake replied seriously. "But he's so immature. That's why Dad sent him to Rome with me. We have to be careful who he associates with."

She bristled. "Dan's mind is nothing to sneeze at. He has an amazing memory. Don't worry, he won't contaminate your brother's intellect."

He regarded her as if taking her measure. "What kind of school do you go to where it's okay to pick up and fly to Europe on the spur of the moment in the middle of the semester?"

"It's an alternative school," Amy lied smoothly.

"And since Dan and I are on our own, it's pretty much up to us if we want to take a trip."

"You're underage," Jake pointed out. "You must have a legal guardian."

Amy swallowed the lump in her throat that formed when she thought of Nellie and Fiske. "We have alternative guardians, too."

Alternative — what a great word to describe the Cahills.

"Are they with you here in Rome?"

For Amy, that question put Jake Rosenbloom over the top. He was entirely too curious. But even if the guy was nothing more than a good-looking snob, she still couldn't risk saying too much. What if Jake got wind of the kidnappings and — with the best of intentions — called the police?

She sped up, leaving Jake behind. "Atticus!" she called. "Which way to the Porta Sanavivaria?"

Atticus beckoned. "Follow me!"

That was another thing about Atticus. He never walked; he ran. Dan was hot on his heels, with Amy and Jake bringing up the rear. He led them to the huge stone arch that was the east entrance to the Colosseum.

"When the games began, the entire procession would march in through the Gate of Life. The gladiators would face the emperor and shout, 'We who are about to die salute you!'"

"Awesome," exclaimed Dan in admiration. "I mean, I wouldn't want to do it myself, but talk about style!"

Atticus was just getting warmed up. "In battle, when

a gladiator had his opponent at his mercy, he would turn to the crowd for thumbs-up or thumbs-down. If the loser was spared, he could leave through the Gate of Life. If it was thumbs-down—"

"Don't tell me," said Amy. "There's a Gate of Death, too."

"Right." The boy genius pointed to the opposite end of the arena, where a similar portal led to the outside. "The Porta Libitinensis—the west entrance, across the way. Now, when the emperor was in attendance, *he* would be the one in charge of who lived and who, you know, didn't. . . ."

Amy glanced at her brother. He was no longer listening. All his attention was focused on a posted diagram just inside the Gate of Life. She recognized the look on his face—one of intense concentration and dawning light. He was on to something, or at least he thought he was.

She sidled over. "What is it?"

"This is a map of the tunnels under the Colosseum directly below us," he murmured. "Notice anything familiar?"

Amy shrugged. "How could I?"

"See the way the passages curve in and around each other? It's the 'Medusa' snake hair. Not just a little bit. Exactly."

Amy was blown away. "Are you saying what I think you're saying?"

Dan nodded. "Caravaggio's 'Medusa' is a map."

CHAPTER 21

Jake's handsome head insinuated itself between brother and sister. "What are you looking at?"

"The tunnels," Amy asked, "are they open to the public?"

"Some are," he replied. "Others haven't been shored up yet."

"How do you get down there?"

"We'll show you," Atticus volunteered.

The Rosenblooms started down a stone ramp to the arena's now open subfloor. Ancient walls hinted at the enclosures where dangerous animals had been kept in readiness. Amy couldn't help but imagine the pens filled with lions, bears, and other wild beasts. One by one, they would be loaded into the hoist and lifted to the arena to do battle with Rome's greatest gladiators for public entertainment. She could almost hear the jungle snarls magnified by the underbelly of the ring, which would have been directly above their heads. And on the other side of that wooden floor—the clash of steel, the crack of bone, the agonized wail of combat and death.

Dan felt it, too. "This might be the coolest place I've ever been."

"I know," chortled Atticus. "The tunnels were originally created to provide access from the Colosseum to other buildings — the Spoliarium, where the dead bodies were taken; the Armamentarium, where the weapons were stored; and the Ludus Magnus, the great gladiator school."

Dan nodded. "Makes sense. If you lose a battle, you get sent back to gladiator school."

Amy let out an exasperated breath. But when she noticed Jake rolling his eyes, she was offended on her brother's behalf. Where did this arrogant jerk get off looking down on Dan, who had heisted Caravaggio's "Medusa" against all odds? *Twice!*

Atticus continued. "The tunnels extend far beyond the walls of the Colosseum, under this entire part of the city. And not all of them have been explored."

Atticus in the lead, they navigated the maze of holding pens and passed through one of many arches that ringed the subfloor. Now they weren't *in* the Colosseum so much as underneath it — in the foundation of one of the world's most barbaric structures.

The only light came from bare bulbs strung far apart, providing just enough illumination to keep visitors from walking into walls. The effect was eerie, but not half as much as it would have been in the time of the Flavian emperors, when these passages had been torch-lit. The floor sloped down as they progressed; a damp chill emanated from the stone. The tourists who had been exploring with them began to thin out. It was one thing to walk in the footsteps of gladiators. But the Colosseum, with its fresh air and sunlight, was far behind them. This place no longer felt like a historic site. It felt like the bowels of the earth.

The atmosphere seemed to be affecting Jake, too. "What do you say we turn around?" he suggested. "I don't think there's anything else up ahead."

"You guys don't have to come with us," Amy said airily. "We can catch up with you back at the Colosseum."

"I want to keep going," Atticus told his brother. "I've never been this far before."

"Because there's nothing to see," Jake grumbled. Yet he shuffled along, bringing up the rear as the group moved on.

When they came to the first fork in the passage, Atticus hesitated, but Dan immediately chose the path to the left and kept on going.

"Wait a minute," Jake protested. "We don't want to get lost down here."

"We can't get lost," Amy replied with exaggerated patience. "Dan has total recall. He's memorized the map of the tunnels, and on the way out, he'll be able to backtrack every twist and turn."

"That's a skill I don't have," said Atticus, impressed.

"It's probably the only one," Dan assured him with a grin.

But he was all business as they navigated the labyrinth past two more intersections.

"Is it the 'Medusa'?" Amy whispered when the Rosenblooms fell back a little. "And the passageways match the snake hair?"

"You bet," Dan confirmed. "The painting is a map, all right."

"With one important detail missing," Amy added. "There's no X-marks-the-spot."

"I've got a theory about that," Dan murmured. "There's a huge tangle of snakes, and they wrap around each other a million times. But there's only one spot where a snake bites another snake. I think *that*'s our X."

"How far away is it?"

"Just a few turns," Dan assured her, picking up the pace. "I see it perfectly in my head."

They took the next fork to the right, hugging the stone wall around the bend. Suddenly, Amy stumbled, somersaulting over a wooden barrier. On it were signs in a dozen languages. The English one read:

UNEXCAVATED—DO NOT ENTER

As Dan was hauling his sister to her feet, the Rosenblooms caught up.

"Well, that's that," Jake announced, an I-told-you-so expression on his face.

"That's nothing," Amy retorted, dabbing at a cut lip. "We're going on."

"The tunnel's closed!" Jake exclaimed.

"No, it's not," Dan said reasonably. "I'm looking straight at it. It's as open as the part we just came through."

Now Jake was annoyed. "Unexcavated means this part of the tunnel isn't safe. That it's not shored up, that it's untested. It could cave in on top of you."

"This tunnel has been here for two thousand years," Dan shot back. "Why would it pick today to cave in?"

Amy tried to play peacemaker. "You guys head back. Dan and I need to explore a little more."

Jake's eyes narrowed. "*Need* to?"

"This is just our hobby," Dan answered quickly. "Instead of collecting stamps, we find creepy old places and poke around." The last part wasn't even a lie. The Clue hunt had taken them through tombs, catacombs, and all manner of buried and secret chambers.

"We understand that it's not for everybody," Amy added soothingly.

Atticus spoke up. "I want to go with Dan."

"No way, Att."

"I've spent my whole life reading books about stuff I never get to see and do!" Atticus argued.

"You don't care about that," Jake accused. "You just can't bear to part with your hero!"

"He's my *friend*!"

"Forget it!"

Amy and Dan watched in amazement as the two brothers got into a heated argument. With symmetrical shrugs, the Cahills left them and ventured into the forbidden section of the tunnel. After rounding the first corner, they could no longer see the Rosenblooms, but they continued to hear Jake laying down the law and Atticus protesting.

"We're still on the snakes, right?" Amy queried.

"Check," Dan confirmed. "Caravaggio had lousy taste in models, but as a mapmaker, the guy rocked. See? The passage should veer to the left and — uh-oh."

They rounded the bend and found themselves staring into blackness. The electric lighting went no farther.

"Now what?" he asked.

Amy dug through her pockets and came up with her flashlight key chain. The beam was faint against such smothering darkness, but it was enough to allow them to go on. They moved more slowly now, stumbling over loose rocks on the tunnel floor.

The passage went on for perhaps another hundred yards and ended abruptly at a T. "This is it," Dan announced.

Amy played the beam around the featureless stone walls. "Here? Really?"

"Exactly here," Dan affirmed. "The end of this path is the biting snake and the cross path is the snake it's biting."

They examined every inch of the intersection. If the

"Medusa" truly was a map, it didn't seem to lead to any treasure.

"They never make it easy," Dan groaned. He picked up a rock and began tapping at the walls, searching for a hollow sound.

"Good idea." Amy reached down for a similar-size stone at her feet. It wouldn't budge. She pulled harder, using both hands. There was movement, not just from the rock but from the ground under her feet.

"Dan—help me out with this."

The two got down on their knees and pulled with all their might. There was a scraping noise, and a large piece of stone floor lifted away. They pushed it aside and turned their attention to the opening it left behind.

In the hollow lay a bundle wrapped in ancient cloth that had mostly disintegrated into its component threads. The material parted under Amy's touch to reveal a rounded piece of cracked and dry wood. When they noted the convex shape, they gazed at each other in wonder.

"It's a shield," Dan breathed. "Just like—"

"Wait a minute!" Amy interrupted. "Remember the legend? Caravaggio's 'Medusa' was supposed to be based on an earlier shield by Leonardo Da Vinci. It was never found—and this is probably the reason why."

She directed her narrow beam of light onto the object. All that remained of the image that had once been painted there were faint shadings on the wood.

"It's gone," Dan observed.

"A lot of Da Vinci's work didn't last," Amy added.

It took a moment to sink in. The shield in her hand had once held an image created by the greatest artist of all time.

She set it down and they turned their attention to the other item in the ragged bundle.

"A book?" mused Dan.

It was a large manuscript, its pages sewn with thick cords and bound into heavy leather covers. Amy opened it to the inside leaf. It was written in elegant calligraphy and fading ink. But what was the language? French? She recognized the word *monde*, which meant *world*. But Amy had studied French, and this wasn't it.

Pounding feet echoed in the tunnel. The Cahills looked up to find a slight figure coming their way. Amy raised the key chain light beam. Atticus.

The younger boy was out of breath. "Whatever you're doing, hurry! Jake went to rat you out to security!"

Amy slammed the manuscript shut, but not before the prodigy had seen the title page. "Where did you get that?"

"What — this?" babbled Dan, searching his mind for an explanation and coming up totally empty.

"It's *The Travels of Marco Polo*!" Atticus breathed reverently.

"No, it isn't," Amy denied. "It's in a weird language — almost like French."

The prodigy dropped to his knees beside them. "It *is* French—*Old* French. The original title was *Books of the Wonders of the World*. In Italian they call it *Il Milione—The Million*." His hands passed delicately and lovingly over a few pages. "This is an astonishing find! How did you know it was here?"

The Cahills' eyes met. They couldn't tell him. No way.

"It's a really long story," Dan offered, "and I promise to explain it to you one day. But not now."

Atticus was too absorbed in the pages to take offense. "There's an epilogue!" he exclaimed in an awed whisper. "Something I've never seen before—and I've read *Il Milione* at least ten times! Do you know what this means? This isn't just an original; it's *Marco Polo's* original—dictated to Rustichello da Pisa at the end of the thirteenth century!"

Amy and Dan shared an instant of perfect understanding. This book and its epilogue were what Vesper One had been after all along—his real reason for compelling them to steal the Caravaggio! The "Medusa" was the map, the back of the shield was the location, and the manuscript was the treasure! Something in that lost epilogue was so valuable to the Vespers that it justified kidnapping and who knew what else.

At that moment, Jake's distant call echoed through the tunnels. "Att—where are you?"

"I'm with Amy and Dan!" the boy genius shouted back. "And you'll never believe what we found!"

"You will return to the legal part of the tunnel!" ordered an authoritative voice, deeper, and with an Italian accent. "At once!"

Atticus stood up, still cradling the Marco Polo manuscript. "I almost hate to give it up. I know it belongs in a museum, but—"

To his utter astonishment, Dan snatched the leather-bound volume right out of his arms.

The boy's smile disappeared as he took in the seriousness and intensity of Dan's expression. "You can't keep it."

"*You* were going to."

"I was only kidding," Atticus told him. "It's a cultural treasure. It belongs to the world."

Protecting the manuscript with crossed arms, Dan made no reply.

Amy set the Da Vinci shield back in its space in the floor and did her best to kick the stone slab into place over it. "We should go," she urged gently.

Dan nodded, but his eyes were filled with regret over the distress he was causing his buddy.

Atticus gawked in escalating dismay. His IQ may have been off the charts, but he could not quite wrap his mind around the fact that Dan was really going to take the manuscript.

"I thought we were friends," he whispered finally.

"We *are* friends."

The young prodigy shook his head sadly. "I'd never

be friends with someone who would steal something like this."

Amy could almost feel the hot shame radiating from her brother. *He's made so few friends since the clue hunt. The admiration of this half-pint Mr. Know-It-All means a lot to him. And now it's gone.*

She sympathized—honestly she did. But nothing took priority over doing what needed to be done.

"Dan—" she prompted.

They heard the slap-slap-slap of rushing feet in the tunnel—Jake and the guard, growing closer.

"I'm sorry, Atticus—" Dan managed.

He turned and ran, the Marco Polo manuscript tucked in the crook of his arm. Behind him, Atticus's high-pitched voice echoed through the tunnels. "Jake! *Jake!*" He seemed to be screaming and sobbing at the same time.

Amy was at Dan's side, holding the flashlight key chain in front of her like a headlamp. "You don't think he's upset enough to get himself lost down here?"

"Don't worry, the guard will find him," Dan panted. "Come on, we've got to beat them back to the Colosseum!"

They could see electric light in the distance—the "legal" part of the tunnel system.

And then a large uniformed man stepped out into their path.

Dan put on the brakes so suddenly that Amy very nearly plowed into him from behind.

"Halt!" ordered the guard.

The Cahills wheeled on a dime and started in the opposite direction. The Clue hunt had honed their escape instinct into a fine art, and the talent served them well here. They sprinted through the passages, turning left and right, weaving an intricate trail through the maze of tunnels.

At last, Dan slowed. It was a mistake. Strong hands reached from a side passage, grasping him firmly under the arms. Dan struggled to get free, but the hold was too powerful.

"*Guardia! Vieni aiuto!*" shouted Jake Rosenbloom.

Atticus was reunited with his brother. His face was streaked with tears. The young genius was barely coherent. "*Il Milione*, Dan . . . *Il Milione* . . ."

Amy's eyes were on Jake. "Let him go," she said quietly.

"Why?" he demanded. "So you can plunder a World Heritage Site?"

"You have no idea what's at stake."

"Do *you*?" Jake retorted. "This is Marco Polo's original manuscript. There's an epilogue that's never been seen before! By anybody! Who do you think you are?"

In a lightning motion, Amy's foot came up, striking Jake in the side of the abdomen, just below the rib cage. He emitted a short gasp as all the air came out of him. His hold on Dan evaporated, and he hit the ground, dazed and winded.

The Cahills fled.

CHAPTER 22

Dan knew the instant they left the "Medusa map," but he didn't stop moving, navigating by the dim glow cast by Amy's key chain light. Loose rubble hampered their progress, and they had to slow down. Here, a twisted or broken ankle would be more than a painful inconvenience. At best, they would be caught by the Italian police. At worst, they would be lost forever in this underground capillary of a dead empire.

Amy grabbed his wrist and the two came to a stop. "Listen," she hissed.

Silence. No shouted threats, no pounding footsteps of pursuit, just their own anxious breathing.

"You think we gave them the slip?" Dan whispered.

"Maybe. Either that or they won't enter the unexcavated part of the tunnels. Why should they? They're assuming we have to come back to the Colosseum sooner or later. All they need to do is wait around and scoop us up."

Dan was alarmed. "We *do* have to go back to the Colosseum sooner or later—don't we?"

"The whole point of digging a tunnel," she reasoned, "is to have a secret passage between point A and point B. There has to be another exit somewhere."

"Aren't you forgetting something?" Dan's voice rose sharply. "This is the Roman Empire—most of the point Bs crumbled to dust centuries ago! Who knows what's there now? This tunnel could lead into the concrete foundation of an eleven-story parking garage!"

"It's a chance we'll have to take." She pointed to the Marco Polo manuscript in his arms. "We need to figure out what the epilogue means. If we get arrested, the police will confiscate the book."

"That's the least of our problems," Dan told her. "How'd you like to miss the 'Medusa' drop-off in Florence because we're sitting in a jail cell in Rome?"

Amy gulped. In the end, it was all about the hostages. No effort could be spared, no corner cut, while there was still an opportunity to bring them home safe and sound. Well, more or less sound.

"What could be in a Marco Polo manuscript that has anything to do with the Vespers?" Dan wondered. "Marco Polo lived in the twelve and early thirteen hundreds—before there were Vespers and Cahills."

"I'm not sure," Amy admitted. "We're assuming that Damien Vesper was interested in something *new*, like Gideon's serum. But what if Vesper was mixed up in something *old*—dating back to Marco Polo's time? Maybe even to the days of Pliny the Younger."

At that moment, Amy's flashlight key chain flickered, and the circle of illumination it cast grew dimmer.

Dan's heart dropped. "Have you got spare batteries for that thing?"

She shook her head sadly. "It's just a freebie they were giving out at the dry cleaners in Attleboro. I never thought I'd actually use it."

The walls were growing closer together, until Dan's narrow shoulders were passing just inches from the rock on both sides, and he had to duck his head in a few places. This was no gladiator's tunnel; it would barely serve as a kindergartner's tunnel. Where could it possibly be leading them?

The beam flickered again, fading to a rusty brown. They forged on, knowing that even if the light died altogether, they'd have no choice but to continue blind, crawling over pebbly debris, feeling for a way out with flailing hands.

It's my fault! Dan berated himself. *I had two years to re-create the serum. Then we could have destroyed the Vespers the minute we heard about the kidnappings. The hostages would be safe, and Amy and I wouldn't be lost in the dark in an ancient Roman tunnel!*

At that instant, the light died utterly. There was no beam, not even a dim glow.

Wild, uncontrollable panic. *We'll die down here! No one will ever find us—*

"Wait a minute—" Amy began.

"What?"

"Our light's out. So—"

He finished her sentence. " — how come I can see you and you can see me?"

Dan blinked. She was right! Sure, it was dark, but without the key chain light, they should have been smothered in blackness. There was light coming from somewhere. And light meant maybe this awful journey was actually going to end.

He got to his feet and stumbled on forward. "This way!"

They picked up the pace, buoyed by the perception that it might be getting just a little bit brighter — or was that just wishful thinking?

All at once, the narrow tunnel opened into a large underground grotto. The sudden absence of walls closing in on him gave Dan a sensation of freedom he hadn't even known he was missing. He looked up. An elaborate domed ceiling hung above them. This was no random underground chamber! It was finished and decorated — at least it had been a zillion years ago.

Amy spun around, taking in her surroundings with a growing sense of amazement and discovery.

"Dan —" Her voice was reverent. "Do you know where we are?"

Dan was impatient. "Wherever it is, how do you get out?"

"I've seen pictures of this place! It's the Lupercal!"

"What's that — some diet pill?"

"In mythology, Rome was founded by two brothers,

Romulus and Remus, who were raised by a she-wolf in a cave. *This* was that cave."

Dan looked skeptical. "Who tiled the ceiling? The wolf?"

"I didn't say it was *true*; I said the ancients believed it. So they turned this place into some sort of shrine. It's under the ruins of Emperor Augustus's house on the Palatine — that's one of the Seven Hills of Rome."

"Who cares about that?" Dan returned. "Where's the door?"

Amy shook her head. "I don't think there is one."

"You said there were pictures."

"The archaeologists dropped a remote camera down a hole in the roof," Amy explained. "The Lupercal grotto hasn't been explored yet. We're the first people to stand in this spot for two thousand years. How incredible is that?"

Dan was unimpressed. "You know what would be even more incredible? An exit sign."

If there was a way out, it was surely inaccessible. The entire far side of the chamber was blocked by a cave-in. Earth and rocks formed a steep slope that soared nearly to the ceiling. Peering up the incline, they could see the light source — a sliver of blue sky where the cave wall met the dome.

Amy pointed. "They must have lowered the camera from there."

There was a distant clinking sound. A tiny pebble dropped from the opening and rolled down the debris pile to land at their feet.

"Somebody's up there!" Dan hissed.

He zipped the Marco Polo manuscript inside his jacket and began to climb the slope. Amy followed, eating loose dirt from her brother's messy progress. Dan got about ten feet off the floor before hitting a soft spot and beginning a slow slide down again. Amy caught his arm, stopping his descent, and the two scrambled together, inching toward the top. The earth mound was so unstable that every few feet would send one of them slithering back. They stayed close, so each could support the other. It was half climbing, half swimming. Their sweat mingled with the earth, covering them with slimy mud.

Dan got in range of the ceiling first. The dome was close enough to touch, and he could see that the mosaic pattern had actually been created with seashells. It was pretty cool, but his one priority was departure. He tried to snake through the opening, but it was just a little too narrow for his shoulders.

I can't fit!

"Hello?" he called.

It got a huge response from the two scientists who were tapping and chiseling into the Lupercal. The pair leaped to their feet and began to back away, mouths agape. Their legs locked, and they went down in a heap. Dan could well understand their shock. When you're painstakingly trying to open an ancient grotto that hasn't seen the light of day for two thousand years, the last thing you expect is some mud-encrusted kid trying to squeeze his way out.

They began to jabber in excited Italian, of which Dan did not understand a single word. He extended his arm, snatched a hammer from the spot where one man had dropped it, and began to hack at the edge of the hole that was blocking his exit. Then he hoisted himself up to the grass of the Palatine Hill.

"How you are in this place that has been sealed since the time of Caesar Augustus?" one of the archaeologists demanded in amazement.

"I was looking for my sister," Dan quipped.

"Your *sister*?"

"Oh—here she is." He reached through the opening and hauled out an equally grubby Amy.

"You will explain your presence here immediately!"

"Sorry. Gotta bounce," Amy said breezily.

The bewildered scientists watched in wonder as the filthy American teens scampered down the Palatine Hill, slaloming around ancient homes and ruins. They were still running when they hit the Via di San Gregorio and disappeared aboard a city bus.

* * *

The taxi driver already had a sour look on his face as he loaded their luggage into the trunk. Amy could read his mind. He was anticipating an endless ride to the airport through the brutal Rome traffic.

If he only knew, she thought.

Dan held out his cell phone, his expression solemn. "You'd better hear this."

Amy raised the handset to her ear just as the voice mail began. *"Hi, Dan, it's Atticus. How's it going? Uh— I guess that's kind of a dumb question because, in actuality, it probably isn't going so good. Jake ratted you out to the police, so by the time you hear this—"*

"Not that one!" she exclaimed suddenly, snatching her overfilled backpack from the driver's hands. It contained one "Medusa" by Caravaggio and one original Marco Polo manuscript—the most sought-after item in the world and a treasure the world did not yet even know existed. Not a bag to let out of your sight. "I'll keep this with me."

"As you wish." The man slammed the trunk shut and opened the rear door.

As they got in, Amy tried to return the phone to her brother, but he handed it back to her. "There's more. He left eleven messages while we were in the tunnels."

"It's me again—Atticus. I feel bad about this. Well, not in actuality, because you did steal Il Milione. *We're still in the police station. There are two Interpol agents coming over to interview us. Interpol, Dan—that's the international police force. . . ."*

The driver got behind the wheel of the taxi. "Destination?"

"Florence," Amy replied.

"Firenze?" the man repeated in amazement. "You

do not travel to Firenze by taxi. It is three hundred kilometers away!"

In answer, Amy pulled a handful of hundred-euro notes from her backpack and dropped them over the bench seat.

The driver started the engine and pulled away from the hotel.

"The Interpol guys didn't believe us about Il Milione, but wait till you hear this: They suspect you and Amy might have been behind that big Caravaggio heist at the Uffizi! They say you were in Florence! Crazy, right? But if you don't turn yourselves in, it's going to look like you've got something to hide, when you're innocent. . . ."

Amy handed back the phone. "Innocent," she said aloud. "I don't even know what that word means anymore."

He accepted it glumly. "That kid hates me now. I guess I can't really blame him."

"If he hated you, he wouldn't be trying to convince you to clear your name," Amy reasoned. "He'd just throw you to the sharks. When this is over, and we're all back in the States, you can explain it to him. He's smart. He'll understand."

"You're dreaming," her brother told her. "There's no such thing as 'when this is over' for our family. We got past the clue hunt, and along came the Vespers. When we get the hostages back, it'll be something else. Trust me, five hundred years of backstabbing was just a warm-up. I'll be able to explain this to Atticus when I can forget . . ." He fell silent, his mind on the seven ingredients to the master serum in his luggage in the trunk.

Amy regarded him with sadness. The chasm between them seemed to grow with each passing day. It wasn't merely that they disagreed; it was that they saw the world with completely different eyes.

Yet in spite of everything that had happened, Amy believed with all her heart that the future could be different. "*We're* the Cahills now—us, Sinead, Ian, Hamilton, Jonah. We're not perfect, but at least we're not trapped in that old thinking. That's what made Grace unique—she was the only one back then who could see *beyond* the clue hunt. She died before she could bring the family to this point, so we have to try to live up to her vision."

A sudden news bulletin interrupted the Euro-pop on the radio in the taxi. Amy and Dan didn't understand the message itself, but there was no mistaking the newscaster's urgency. Amy's heart sank as she recognized the words *Colosseo, Caravaggio, Uffizi, Americano,* and *Cahill.* She watched as the driver's shoulders stiffened, and his eyes darted to the rearview mirror.

She plucked another few hundred-euro notes from the backpack and tossed them to the front seat. "A bonus," she said, "for speed."

The man gave an elaborate European shrug and stepped on the gas.

CHAPTER 23

The test was conducted in the main room of the Vesper holding cell. Fiske, Alistair, Reagan, Natalie, and Phoenix each brandished a piece of plastic cutlery to determine which of them had the steadiest hand.

"It would appear," Fiske decided, "that young Phoenix is our 'winner.'"

The boy turned white as a sheet. "Me? I can't cut Nellie! What if I do something wrong?"

"What if we do nothing at all?" Fiske countered.

"Let me do it!" Reagan exclaimed. "My hand is as steady as anybody's."

Alistair shook his head. "I admire your courage, child. But Phoenix has the touch that's required."

"Just so long as I don't have to," Natalie quavered, wrapping herself in her own arms. "The whole thing is so—medieval!"

Nellie's weak voice came from the bedroom. "I'm shot; I'm not deaf." She had been drifting in and out of consciousness as her fever rose and fell.

"All right, I'll do the surgery," Phoenix agreed. "But someone has to tell me every move."

"You have my word," Fiske promised. He did not bother to mention that removing the scalpel from the dumbwaiter had been the first time he'd ever touched one.

They tore apart a sheet to make bandannas that served as surgical masks. The bed was their operating table, simply because no one had the courage to move the patient. Phoenix entered the room, his hands as washed and sterilized as he could make them.

It was time.

Nellie did her best to smile at him. "You can do this, kiddo." She watched his eyes fill with tears. "And no crying. You have to see what you're doing."

He picked the scalpel off the tray and Nellie bit hard on the gag in her mouth. It was all the comfort she was going to get. This operation would be without anesthesia.

Phoenix was amazed at how easily the scalpel cut through flesh. The gag muffled Nellie's cry of pain. She tried to squirm away, but Reagan pressed her down to the mattress, keeping her firmly in place. Blood covered the incision, and Fiske mopped it away with a fistful of the sheet fabric.

"A second cut," Alistair suggested, observing from a step back so his twitching arm wouldn't jostle Phoenix. "Forming an X. It will open wider and allow you to get inside."

And although he wasn't sure he could even hold the scalpel, Phoenix did as he was told. More blood. He felt the top of his head rising toward the ceiling and fought it back down again.

Of course there's blood! When you cut people, they bleed!

He had to keep it together. Everybody was counting on him.

"Tweezers," Fiske instructed, none too steady himself.

Almost in slow motion, Phoenix set the bloody scalpel down and picked up the tweezers. He could hear Nellie's moaned complaint as he probed into the flesh of her torn shoulder.

"I don't feel it," he said, hysteria rising.

"Move the instrument around," Fiske coached. "Gently."

Phoenix was sweating now. He could feel the moisture pouring down his face, stinging his eyes. On the other side of the bed, Ted had gotten up from his chair and was pacing the room, hugging the wall. Natalie was curled up in a corner, whimpering. Even Reagan had lost her Holt bravado and was looking on in awe and dread.

All at once, Phoenix became aware of something small and hard coming into contact with one tip of the tweezers. "There it is!"

"Excellent," Fiske approved. "Now pull it out slowly."

Phoenix worked his wrist and fingers. "I can't get a grip on it."

"Keep trying," Alistair encouraged.

Desperately, Phoenix attempted to maneuver both tips of the instrument around the bullet. He knew that each move caused Nellie unimaginable pain, but he could not grasp the target. "It's no use," he sobbed. "And my hand is going numb."

In a frenzy, Nellie shouted something into the gag, but no one could understand her.

"I beg your pardon, child?" queried Alistair.

Nellie spat out the rag and rasped, "Get the Kabra chick!"

"Natalie?" Fiske exclaimed. "She's fallen completely to pieces."

"Get her!" Nellie demanded. "Anybody with eyebrows plucked like that knows how to use a tweezers!"

Reagan bounded across the room and came back with a shivering, mewling Natalie.

"I can't!" she wheezed.

Fiske poured alcohol over the girl's beautifully manicured fingers. "You must."

Still protesting, her eyes tightly shut, she took over the instrument from Phoenix. "I can't do it! You can't make me—oh!" she said in sudden surprise. "This?" And when she pulled the tweezers out of the wound, the tips were firmly grasping a flattened, blood-slimed bullet.

Nellie laughed—and promptly fainted.

CHAPTER 24

The hulking SUV's headlights illuminated rocky terrain and endless trees. The Sentinel range of upstate New York's Adirondack Mountains was paradise for winter skiers and summer boaters and hikers. But it was a navigator's nightmare, with narrow winding roads and few signs.

Ian Kabra rolled up his window. "My God, what's that smell?"

Behind the wheel, Sinead laughed. "It's called fresh air. Growing up in London, you've probably never breathed it before."

"And I hope I never breathe it again," Ian said feelingly. "Who would put a mobile phone factory where the closest civilization is a petrol station thirty miles away?"

"Someone who wants to keep his factory top secret," came William McIntyre's voice over the SUV's Bluetooth communications system. He and Evan Tolliver were monitoring the quartet's progress from the attic of Grace's house. "Whether DeOssie Industries is connected to the Vespers, or Vesper One is merely a client, a low profile serves the company and its customers well."

Jonah emitted a loud yawn. "Are we there yet, yo?"

"Are we boring you, Jonah?" Sinead demanded. "I apologize if rescuing our hostages isn't cool enough to get you on *Entertainment Tonight*."

The star straightened in his seat. "What I'm saying is, I've got my game face on, and I'm good to go. Enough playing around—let's find our people and end this *tonight*!"

Hamilton leaned forward and gave the GPS system a flick with his sausagelike finger. "This thing must be busted. Either that or we're going someplace that doesn't exist."

"Impossible," Sinead said confidently. "We're running off the *Gideon* satellite. We get occasional interference from the aurora borealis, but I haven't seen that for a few weeks."

They crested a rise, and there it was, in the hollow between rolling hills—a low, square building, ghostly gray in the moonlight.

"Is that it?" asked Hamilton.

"It probably isn't the local opera house," groaned Ian.

"Why's it so empty?" Jonah wondered.

"It *is* after midnight," Sinead pointed out.

"That's weird," Evan commented from the comm. center. "A place like that should never be completely deserted. They'd have security."

"The parking lot's a ghost town," Hamilton supplied. "And the factory's dead black."

"That's a good thing," Sinead reminded them. "After all, we're breaking in."

They left the SUV in a gap in the trees and approached the main gate cautiously on foot. As Sinead turned her attention to the security keypad, Hamilton leaned against the fencing, which swung wide under his weight.

"Yo," mused Jonah, "would you buy secure technology from a fool who doesn't remember to lock his own gate?"

"It is highly irregular," came McIntyre's voice, now from their cell phones. "Proceed with caution."

It was eerie walking by flashlight through acres of parking lot without a single vehicle in sight.

Jonah spoke what everybody was thinking. "Wouldn't it be Twilight Zone if the door was open, too?"

Hamilton tried the knob. It didn't budge.

Ian stepped forward and examined the lock. "Natalie's diary has better security than this." He produced a credit card and slipped it between the latch and the jamb. There was a click, and the door swung wide.

The foursome tensed for the wail of an alarm. It didn't happen.

They scanned the walls and ceiling for motion detectors and surveillance cameras. There was nothing. Sinead produced a small spray bottle and pumped a cloud of water vapor into the air. No geometric grid of red laser lines appeared. In fact, there seemed to be no security at all.

Hamilton held up his cell phone to stream a view of the office to the comm. center. "You guys see anything we don't?"

Four flashlight beams played around the room. There were identical employee cubicles, a coffee station, water cooler, and snack machine. Productivity charts and job assignment boards covered the walls.

"It looks like where Dilbert works," was Evan's comment.

"Word," Jonah agreed. "If I had to nine-to-five it in a place like this, I'd off myself."

"Not everyone lives the high life, Jonah," McIntyre reminded him gently.

"I did once," Ian said wistfully. "Those were the days."

"Let's keep our heads in the game," Sinead suggested. "Look at this place—there's still work on the desks, pictures of people's kids—"

"Here's a half-eaten sandwich," put in Hamilton. "I wonder if it's still good."

"The snack machine is stocked," Sinead went on, "the assignment board is up-to-date. What hit this place?"

"Maybe nothing," Ian mused. "Could be they'll be back to their pathetic little jobs in the morning all right and tight."

"No chance," Evan interjected from Attleboro. "There should be cleaning crews and at least one night watchman. These people provide phones to the CIA! It's not reasonable that they'd leave the place unattended like this."

"You think we're being set up?" asked Jonah.

"Not necessarily," Ian reasoned. "Futuristic mobile phones, futuristic security. Just because we can't see it doesn't mean it isn't here."

"It doesn't matter," Sinead decided. "Security or not, trap or not, the hostages could be as close as a secret compartment, maybe even right under our feet. We have to search this place, and I mean inch by inch."

The four began a methodical sweep of the building—every drawer, every closet, every file cabinet. From the office, they moved to the factory floor, past workstations, conveyor belts, and towering shelves of raw materials. They operated mostly in silence, holding ultrasensitive sound detectors, hoping to catch a hint of speech or movement coming from some remote or hidden area of the building.

"Freeze!" Evan exclaimed suddenly. "One of you—Hamilton, I think—take a step back! There—in the bin on the middle shelf."

Hamilton moved his cell phone closer to provide a better view. "This one?"

"Jackpot! Sinead—go and have a look. I think that's the missing charger we've been working on."

In less than a minute, Sinead was at Hamilton's side. She stared into the bin. "Great. I'll grab a bunch so we've got some spares."

"Yeah, great," Hamilton echoed without much enthusiasm. He had come here to rescue Reagan and the others. A charger seemed a poor substitute, because he was beginning to doubt there was anyone to be found in this place.

For half an hour they scoured the facility without result. There was a bitter truth to be faced. The hostages were not here, nor was there any clue linking this deserted factory to the Vespers. This had been a good guess, but the wrong one.

Depressed and defeated, they reassembled in the office.

Even Ian was surprised by the depth of his disappointment. "There's only one thing worse than coming to a wasteland like this, and that's coming here for nothing."

"At least we got the chargers," Sinead sighed. "We can send a couple to Amy and Dan in the morning. Let's get back to the car."

Hamilton approached the snack dispenser. "I'm going to grab some Cheez Doodles for the ride home. My dad taught me this — watch." He wrapped his massive arms around the machine and tipped it up slightly. Then he made a product choice with his elbow and smashed his head against the coin slot. Chip bags began to rain down.

"Sick skills, cuz," Jonah approved. "Pick me up a Baby Ruth—"

An enormous explosion rocked the building on its foundation.

"Hit the deck!" cried Sinead.

The four dropped to the floor just as a wave of flame passed over them, searing them with its heat. There was a second blast and the file cabinets against the far wall disappeared in a fireball.

"The door!" Ian croaked.

They were halfway there when a series of charges went off in front of them, blocking the exit. More explosions detonated all around. And then an even more terrifying sound—the roar of a fire blazing out of control.

"The factory!" Sinead howled, leading the rush from the burning office down the four steps to the manufacturing plant.

But no sooner had their feet touched the concrete floor than a massive blast took out the storage shelving, sending a barrage of burning electronic components raining down on them. From all four cell phones came the frantic voices of McIntyre and Evan.

"What's going on?"

"We've lost you!"

No one could hear the words from Attleboro as a cannonade of explosions engulfed the entire factory.

One by one, the handsets went dead.

"This is *not cool*!" croaked Jonah in a voice none of his fans would have recognized.

A piece of suspended ceiling tile landed on Ian's shoulder and he had to shrug off his jacket and beat the fire out.

The flames towered over them, growing ever closer, sucking the oxygen out of the air. Breathing became difficult as smoke and glowing embers billowed around them.

"How do we get out of here?" Hamilton gasped.

They stood, paralyzed with shock — all but Sinead Starling. The brilliant Ekat ran for a large forklift parked nearby. She jumped behind the wheel just as a heavy piece of metal shelving hit the floor right where she'd been standing a split second before. A turn of the key, and the tow motor roared to life.

She steered for the others, shouting, *"Get in — now!"*

Ian, Hamilton, and Jonah piled into the cab, nearly crushing the driver. They were already picking up speed, rolling through the inferno.

"Are you crazy?" Ian squealed. "There's no way out!"

"We can't stay here!" Sinead kept on driving, shoulders hunched over the controls. They squeezed together even closer in an attempt to avoid the flames that surrounded them on all sides.

At last, her destination became clear — the metal overhead door of the factory's loading bay.

"You're losing it!" Jonah rasped. "We're not going to get through that!"

The forklift's top speed was perhaps ten miles per hour, but amid the maelstrom of smoke and fire, it felt like they were barreling out of control.

"Hang on!" Sinead ordered.

A bare instant before impact, a final explosion blew the heavy gate clean off. It toppled outward, forming a ramp from the loading bay down to the driveway. The forklift rumbled down the broken door to ground level and keeled over on its side.

The four occupants wriggled out and hit the pavement running.

In the comm. center in Attleboro, Evan whipped out his cell phone and dialed 911. "I need the police and the fire department!" he babbled. "In upstate New York! The nearest town is—"

In a single motion, William McIntyre snatched the handset away, threw it to the floor, and ground it to pieces with his heel.

Evan was aghast. "What did you do that for? Now the cops won't know where to go!"

"Precisely," the lawyer said calmly.

"But our people need help!" Evan wailed. "They could get killed!"

"Amy was right," McIntyre told him. "You are not a Cahill. Or you would know that Cahill business is not a matter for the police or the fire department or any other outside organization. There are hostages to be considered, and snooping from the authorities could add to their danger."

Evan stared, his heart thumping against his rib cage. What had he gotten himself into when he'd become involved with Amy Cahill?

— ✳ — ✳ —

The four cousins, scorched and disheveled, watched from the deserted parking lot as the DeOssie factory burned to the ground.

"That was some hard-core James Bond back there." Jonah praised Sinead, his voice trembling despite years of vocal training. "How did you know the door was going to blow?"

She looked at him, shamefaced. "I didn't. I just figured it was better than burning." She pulled a fistful of cell phone chargers out of her pocket. "It's a good thing we took these. I don't think we're going to be able to order replacements anytime soon."

Hamilton opened the snack bag that was still in his shaking hand. He popped a Cheez Doodle into his mouth. "Hey, are these barbecue flavor?"

"They are now," Ian told him.

"We all would be, if it wasn't for Sinead," Jonah pointed out. "This is the last time I underestimate Vesper One. When homey sets a trap, he's not playing."

There was a loud bang, and a window blew, glass spraying uncomfortably close. They all hurried toward the gate and their SUV.

Ian, limping a little, lagged behind. A small scrap of charred paper blew from the wreckage and landed at his feet.

He would have ignored it but for the insignia in the corner of the torn page. It was unmistakable to him — two snake heads on a red crest, the symbol of the Lucian branch of the Cahill family.

Ian's branch.

He picked it up and jammed it into his pocket.

CHAPTER 25

Their last hotel in Florence, the Ilario, had been awarded five stars and was celebrated as the finest in the city. Their current lodging was not mentioned in the guidebook and didn't even have a name.

The sign read CAMERE, which meant, simply, *rooms*. Sandwiched between a pawn shop and a sewage treatment plant, it offered neither maid service nor a working elevator. What it did offer — besides cockroaches of remarkable size — was anonymity. No passports were required at check-in. Few questions were asked of the young American girl traveling with an even younger American boy. Fake names were completely acceptable. Amy and Dan Cahill were wanted by Interpol; Mark and Caroline Farley were merely handed the key to room 6.

The Ilario may have offered luxury, but for two fugitives, there was no luxury like being invisible.

"Well, it's done." Dan stepped out of the bathroom, wearing a forlorn expression. Thick tortoiseshell glasses—the lenses clear—dominated his features. A New York Yankees cap was pulled down low over his brow. He caught a glimpse of his reflection in the tarnished mirror. "I'm a dork. No, worse—I'm a Yankees fan! Don't they have Red Sox hats in Italy?"

"You think I'm thrilled about it?" Amy shot back. She, too, had changed her appearance with a voluminous platinum blond wig. "I look like an escapee from the eighties, not Interpol." She held up a jar of Insta-Tan. "We can darken our complexions with this stuff. Every little bit helps."

"Wouldn't it be simpler to just, you know, get arrested?" Dan caught her sharp expression. "I'm kidding!"

"We're really close," Amy told him. "The drop-off should be today. Once the hostages are safe, we can work on figuring out what the Marco Polo manuscript means."

"If the Marco Polo thingy is what Vesper One really wants," Dan mused, "maybe we should give him that, too."

"No way," Amy said evenly. "Not till we understand the importance of that epilogue."

"It's in some crazy dead language," Dan protested.

"Surely Atticus isn't the only one who can read it. We'll hire a translator."

Dan was uneasy. "If Vesper One finds out we're keeping it from him—"

"It's a chance we'll have to take," Amy insisted.

"That manuscript holds the key to what the Vespers are up to. I'd bet my life on it."

Dan did not reply. He wasn't interested in the other Vespers, but he had declared war on Vesper One the instant he'd seen the video clip of Nellie's shooting. As soon as the hostages were free, he was going to devote himself to finding the rest of the thirty-nine ingredients to Gideon Cahill's master serum. That would be the only weapon he needed.

Their attention was focused on the Vesper phone and its rapidly dwindling power bars, so the Cahills were taken aback when the ringtone sounded from Amy's cell.

Dan read the small screen. "Grace's house? Isn't it, like, four A.M. in Attleboro?"

Amy picked up the handset. "What's up?"

"There's been an incident," came Ian's clipped accent.

"At the DeOssie factory?" Amy asked eagerly. "Were the hostages there?"

"No. And as of now, neither is the DeOssie factory. And it's all because of the Tomas and his Cheez Doodles—"

"Amy, it's Sinead," a businesslike voice broke in. "Let me give you the scoop."

Amy set her phone on speaker, and she and Dan listened to the tale of the assault on the factory in upstate New York.

"A trap!" Dan breathed.

"Definitely," Sinead finished. "So please tell Hamilton to calm down. It wasn't the Cheez Doodles. Those fire bombs would have gone off for Fritos, too, and maybe even Pop Tarts. The whole place was wired to blow. Something would have set it off."

"The good news is we scored your cell phone charger," Jonah put in. "I'm sending my pilot with a bunch of them."

"I hope you're wasting your money," Amy told him honestly. "We're waiting to hear from Vesper One about how to deliver the 'Medusa.' With any kind of luck, this will be all over before your plane lands."

"Ames," came a timid voice. Evan. "Are you okay?"

She smiled in spite of herself. It felt good to be someone's top priority. Perhaps that was selfish with seven hostages in danger, but at that moment Amy was too exhausted to care. "I'm fine, Evan. Just a little—blond. Like Lady Gaga. Don't worry, it isn't permanent. Oh, yeah, and Interpol is after us. We'll have to explain later. The Vesper phone just beeped."

She cut the connection and joined Dan at the DeOssie unit. They waited as the message downloaded and appeared, flickering alarmingly, on the now-dim screen.

```
What fun to visit the circus—especially
when you sit in section 5, row W, seat
11. All the world loves a clown!
```

You are now out of time. Bring the
merchandise. This is your last chance.

Cotton candy is optional.

Vesper One

An advertisement appeared for the Circo di Milano,
performing in the Piazza dei Cinque Fratelli at eight
o'clock that night.

Dan looked uneasy. "If the Vespers are willing to
burn down a whole factory, who knows what they'll
do to a circus."

"If they burn us, they burn the 'Medusa,'" Amy reasoned. "Anyway, we've got no choice."

Piazza dei Cinque Fratelli was a huge open space, well
south of the Arno. Right in the center towered Circo di
Milano's big top, surrounded by smaller tents housing
minor exhibits, food stalls, and carnival games.

"You know," said Dan as they took their place in line
behind a group of excited children and their parents,
"this almost feels like normal life. We're going to the
circus."

"Only this time, we're carrying a stolen masterpiece
in a green garbage bag," Amy reminded him.

"And we're wanted by the cops," Dan added,
inclining his head in the direction of a uniformed

officer standing watch over the main entrance.

The Cahills kept their faces downcast as they approached the ticket window. Yes, their appearance was different now. But it was possible that their pictures had been circulated all over the world. They were a boy and girl of exactly the right age and nationality. And some people were observant enough to look beyond blond hair, phony glasses, and Insta-Tan.

With a sinking heart, Amy realized she would have to betray her American accent in order to buy tickets. Was the officer close enough to hear?

Dan stepped in front of her, slapped a fifty-euro note onto the counter, and held up two fingers. He smiled at the policeman as he accepted his change. The cop smiled back.

Inside the big top, they knew another tense moment — what if Vesper One's seats were already occupied? They needn't have worried. Row W was high up in the stands, and most of the audience wanted to be closer to the ring. Amy took number 11, the wrapped "Medusa" held firmly on her lap.

"How do you think the drop-off is going to happen?" Dan wondered. "You can't get a motorcycle gang up these stairs."

Amy shrugged nervously. "I'm not looking forward to it." At that moment, she knew, she would be face-to-face with an enemy — an agent of the Vespers, who very well might take the package with one hand

and with the other plunge a knife into her chest. "I just hope it goes smoothly and the hostages are all okay."

"Especially Nellie," Dan added.

As showtime approached, the grandstand began to fill, and excited chatter rose in the big top. At last, the circus began, as most circuses do, with a troupe of clowns.

Amy sat forward suddenly. "'All the world loves a clown,'" she quoted.

"I don't," Dan commented. "My favorite part is when the guy in the white glitter suit steps in the elephant poop."

"No—I mean from Vesper One's message! I'll bet one of the clowns will come up here for the handoff."

They watched the clowns closely, squinting into faces, trying to determine if any of them were staring up at section 5, row W, seat 11. But soon the troupe was backstage, replaced by the first act, a tightrope walker.

She was followed by show horses, a lion tamer, a trapeze act, and a trick motorcycle rider. Throughout all this, the clowns came out and meandered around the ring, juggling and performing comedy routines. They entered the stands occasionally but never in the Cahills' direction.

"Are we sitting in the right place?" Amy wondered. "What if we misread the instructions?"

"I'm not the forgetting type," Dan reminded her.

Next was the human cannonball. They could tell that he was one of the biggest stars in the show. He received a standing ovation, and the proceedings paused while he stopped to sign autographs for some of the younger children in the front rows. At last, he donned his helmet, waved to the crowd, and slipped inside the mouth of the cannon in the spotlight's glare. Another spot — this one clear across the arena — shone on the net where the brave performer would land.

The boom was deafening. In a blast of flame, the human cannonball sailed across the big top, landing safely in his net. At that very instant, one of the trapeze artists swung down above Amy, hanging on by her feet. For an instant she was right in front of them, backlit by the cannon's flash — young, dark-haired, and resplendent in a spangled blue costume. A split second later, she snatched the "Medusa" right out of Amy's grasp and rose skyward with it.

CHAPTER 26

Amy and Dan looked up, but by then the trapeze artist was just one of dozens of figures in the spaghetti of ropes and ladders high above the ring. Of the dark bag with the Caravaggio, there was no sign.

"The drop-off!" Amy rasped.

"While we were watching the human cannonball!" Dan added in wonder.

And then, in the midst of the applause for the last act, every single light in the big top went out.

It was different from the various lighting effects of the show. This was a total power failure — suffocating blackness. It took seconds for the smallest children to panic. As they began to run around, the danger became very real. Soon adults began chasing after their kids, and there was the sound of bodies falling. Cries rang out as the chaos escalated.

"Let's get out of here!" Dan urged.

"Right!"

Dan had perfect recall of the route they had followed to their seats. Even so, the path was treacherous, as alarmed patrons were tripped up by darting children and stumbling parents. Somewhere on the floor, the ringmaster was shouting instructions. But without his microphone, no one could hear him.

They reached the bottom of the grandstand, where the pushing and shoving was worst. Dan took an elbow to the jaw and ducked down below the level of the flailing arms, pulling his sister with him. They crawled under the bleachers toward the main entrance, free of the struggling throng. It was Amy who spotted the emergency exit — really just a tent flap held in place by ropes and pegs. They wriggled out through the hole, finding themselves in a dimly lit alley on the periphery of the Piazza dei Cinque Fratelli.

The Cahills got to their feet, dusting themselves off.

"Man," marveled Dan. "Vesper One may be a jerk, but you've got to give him props for setting up a clean drop-off."

"I don't give him 'props' for anything," Amy growled.

A piteous moan reached them, almost at their feet. They looked down to see a petite brunette in a sequined blue costume lying on the pavement.

Dan recognized her immediately. "The trapeze artist!" He held out a hand to help her up. She made no move to take it. Her expression seemed bewildered, eyes wide, lips parted. She tried to speak but could summon no sound.

"It's okay," Amy reassured her. "We know why

you took the package. We understand."

"Amy—" Dan exclaimed in hushed horror.

She followed his pointing finger to the smashed glass syringe on the pavement beside the trapeze artist. A mark on her neck, bleeding slightly, told the tale. Minutes ago, she had performed a service for Vesper One. And this was her reward.

"Who did this to you?" Amy asked urgently.

The girl—barely conscious—tried to raise herself up, but she could not find the strength. Her lips moved, but very little sound came out.

Amy and Dan leaned closer.

With effort, the dying acrobat ran a hand along her bare arm. *"Bru—bru—ciato,"* she barely whispered.

"Bruciato?" Amy repeated, tense with discovery. "I know that word! *Bruciato* means burned or seared."

"Burned?" Dan echoed. "You mean the guy who did this. He had a burn on his arm?"

"She needs a doctor!" Amy leaped up and started for the mouth of the alley. But before she could call for help, the trapeze artist gave a slight shudder.

Then the young woman seemed to collapse in upon her own tiny frame, eyes still open yet suddenly lifeless.

Dan choked on a rush of terror. "Is she —?"

"Somebody call an ambulance! *Ambulanza!*" Amy was aware that she was screaming, but she couldn't stop herself. She could feel hysteria rising. Another innocent person dead, thanks to the Cahills! When would it end? "Help! Somebody help!"

Dan grabbed her and hustled her out of the alley. "Cut it out! The last thing we need is to be interviewed by cops! If anybody runs our names through a computer, the Interpol warrant will come up!"

"We need to get her to a hospital!" Amy wailed.

"No hospital can help her, Amy! She's dead!"

It came as a shock in spite of the fact that Amy already knew. "We killed her! Oh, God, Dan, what did that poor girl ever do to us?"

"We didn't kill her," Dan said sternly. "The Vespers did. They kill a lot of people. If that bullet had been three inches to the right, they would have killed Nellie, too."

"At least Nellie knows what she's part of!" Amy blubbered. "This girl was *nobody*! So she took a few euros from a guy with a burn on his arm to pluck a package out of somebody's lap! She didn't deserve to *die* for it!"

People began to stream onto the scene around the side of the tent, and a police whistle shrilled nearby. It jarred Amy back to reality. Falling to pieces would not bring the trapeze artist back. Nothing would.

The drop-off had been made. Next on the agenda: the release of the hostages. The ball was in Vesper One's court now.

They left the Piazza dei Cinque Fratelli, crossing several streets as they put some distance between the circus and themselves. Amy had her arm up about to hail a taxi when the chime of the Vesper phone erased all other thoughts from their minds.

She pulled the device from her pocket, and they examined the screen.

```
Package received. You are too kind.
```

"That's it?" Dan exploded. "What about our people, you murdering psycho?"

As if in answer, a second message came in. It was a photograph of the hostages in the Vesper holding cell.

CAM 4: OUR GUESTS

Seven hostages, Amy counted. *All seven, present and accounted for.*

Nellie was propped up on the floor, a blood-soaked bandage wrapped around her wounded shoulder. She looked pale and weak, her makeup smeared. Brown was now clearly visible at the roots of her dyed black-and-orange hair.

But she's alive. . . .

Amy set aside her relief and read on:

```
Perhaps you notice that your loved ones
continue to accept our hospitality. This
is due to your previous treachery. They
will remain our guests until you complete
a few more tasks. The first of these will
be in Lucerne, Switzerland. Get yourselves
there immediately, lest the number of our
little party dwindles.
```

```
It is a pleasure to continue to work with
such talented young people. Although,
Amy, I much prefer you as a brunette.
```

```
Vesper One
```

"We had a deal!" Dan was red-faced and shaking with rage. "Give me that phone!" He snatched the handset and began to thumb an angry reply on the tiny keypad.

Amy was as quiet as her brother was loud. "It's no use. The texts don't go through, remember?"

"Maybe this one will," he snapped stubbornly.

As he typed, the small screen gave a final flicker and went dark. The Vesper phone was dead.

Amy tried to be encouraging. "We'll have the new charger soon."

"What if there's a new message right now?" Dan raved. "Like, *'Just kidding!'*"

"We don't know much about Vesper One, but we know this: He doesn't kid. The guy is one hundred percent serious." She looked around uneasily. "He saw me. He's here somewhere. I'll bet he murdered that poor girl personally, just for the fun of it."

"Let's get him!" Dan roared, twirling about, scanning the streets.

"We can't."

"He's got a burn on his arm and he's carrying the 'Medusa' in a garbage bag! How hard can it be to find him?"

Amy put her hand on his shoulder to calm him. Inside, she was just as agitated and furious as her brother, but she had to think for both of them. Rash action would never succeed against a cold, calculating adversary like Vesper One. The only Cahill who'd ever come close to understanding the Vespers had been Grace.

Fine. She had to think like Grace.

What would Grace do now?

"Vesper One had this whole thing planned, from the kidnappings to the tiniest detail of tonight," she reasoned. "There's no way he'd leave himself open to being attacked in the street. And even if we could reach him, he's still got our hostages."

"Because he cheated us!" Dan seethed.

"We should have seen that coming," Amy agreed.

"He won't release them until we've got something he needs in return."

"That was supposed to be the 'Medusa'!" Dan argued. "And he still stiffed us. And these new tasks? He'll just stiff us again! Why should we break our necks to follow his orders?"

"It keeps our hostages alive," Amy explained. *"And* it keeps Vesper One believing we're dancing to his tune."

"We *are* dancing to his tune if he calls all the shots!"

"Maybe," Amy replied. "But the Vespers aren't doing this because they're art lovers. They have a grand design—and the extra page in the Marco Polo manuscript is part of it. What's the connection? We've got the full resources of the Cahill family researching the Vespers twenty-four-seven. When we understand what they're *really* up to, *then* we'll know what we can trade for our people. And *we'll* be the ones in charge."

Dan listened to his sister's words, yet part of him was no longer paying attention. *That* Dan had left the streets of Florence and was descending to the dark place in the depths of his mind.

It was a regular hangout for him now—a memory bank where thirty-nine ingredients boiled.

The formula he used to pray he could forget.

The formula he now understood was part of his destiny.

Amy was smart, and her thinking made sense. But Dan had a backup plan, a secret weapon.

Gideon Cahill's serum.

CHAPTER 27

The taxi driver breathed a sigh of relief as Amy Cahill lowered her arm and turned her attention to the smartphone in her pocket. He hadn't really been looking for a fare tonight anyway. He was far more concerned with getting the precious package that lay on the passenger seat beside him to a safe place.

He ran a finger along his sleeve and felt the scar that stretched from shoulder to wrist. It still itched sometimes, even so many years after the unfortunate accident that had burned him. An accident that could be laid at the doorstep of the hated Cahill family.

He passed another potential customer, ignoring the woman's waving hand. He was not a real taxi driver. It was just a cover. He'd had dozens of them, just as he'd had dozens of aliases — although none was as important as the name he had assumed for this, the greatest project of his life.

He called himself Vesper One.

GREETINGS, CAHILLS!

Feel like some breaking and entering? Because I have a teeny little errand for you in Switzerland with my friend de Virga. You'd better head out quickly. I still hold seven of your friends, and my trigger finger is feeling mighty itchy.

Vesper One